DEAD POETS SOCIETY

"Mr. Keating?" Neil called after him. "Sir? O Captain! My Captain?" Keating stopped and waited for the boys to catch up with him. "What was the Dead Poets Society, sir?" Neil asked. For a split second, Keating's face reddened. "I was just looking in an old annual." Neil explained, "and . . ."

"Nothing wrong with research," Keating said, regaining his composure.

The boys waited for him to say more. "But what was it?" Neil pressed.

Keating looked around to make sure that no one was watching. "A secret organization," he almost whispered. "I don't know how the present administration would look upon it, but I doubt the reaction would be favorable." His eyes scanned the campus as the boys held their breaths. "Can you boys keep a secret?"

DEAD POETS SOCIETY

A NOVEL BY N. H. KLEINBAUM

HYPERION

LOS ANGELES • NEW YORK

For information address Hyperion,
77 West 66th Street, New York, New York 10023.

Mass market ISBN 978-1-4013-0877-3
FAC-025438-24064

First edition
31 33 35 36 34 32 30
Printed in the United States of America

DEAD
POETS
SOCIETY

CHAPTER 1

Inside the stone chapel of Welton Academy, a private school nestled in the remote hills of Vermont, more than three hundred boys, all wearing the academy blazer, sat on either side of the long aisle, surrounded by proud-faced parents, and waited. They heard the reverberations of the bagpipes as a short, elderly man swathed in flowing robes lit a candle and led a procession of students carrying banners, robed teachers, and alumnae down a long slate hallway into the venerable chapel.

The four boys who carried banners marched solemnly to the dais, followed slowly by the elderly men, the last of whom proudly carried the lighted candle.

Headmaster Gale Nolan, a husky man in his early sixties, stood at the podium watching expectantly as the procession concluded.

"Ladies and gentlemen . . . boys . . ." he said dramatically, pointing toward the man with the candle. "The light of knowledge."

The audience applauded politely as the older gentleman stepped slowly forward with the candle. The bagpiper marched in place at the corner of the dais, and the four banner carriers, lowering their flags that read, "Tradition," "Honor," "Discipline," and "Excellence," quietly took seats with the audience.

The gentleman with the candle walked to the front of the audience where the youngest students sat holding unlit candles. Slowly, he bent forward, lighting the candle of the first student on the aisle.

"The light of knowledge shall be passed from old to young," Headmaster Nolan intoned solemnly, as each boy lit the candle of the student sitting next to him.

"Ladies and gentlemen, distinguished alumni, and students . . . This year, 1959, marks the hundreth year that Welton Academy has been in existence. One hundred years ago, in 1859, forty-one boys sat in this room and were asked the same question that now greets you at the start of each semester." Nolan paused dramatically, his gaze sweeping the room full of intense, frightened young faces.

"Gentlemen," he bellowed, "what are the four pillars?"

The shuffle of feet broke the tense silence as the

students rose to attention. Sixteen-year-old Todd Anderson, one of the few students not wearing the school blazer, hesitated as the boys around him rose to their feet. His mother nudged him up. His face was drawn and unhappy, his eyes dark with anger. He watched silently as the boys around him shouted in unison, "Tradition! Honor! Discipline! Excellence!"

Nolan nodded, and the boys sat down. When the squeaking of chairs subsided, a solemn hush fell over the chapel.

"In her first year," Dean Nolan bellowed into the microphone, "Welton Academy graduated five students." He paused. "Last year we graduated fifty-one students and over 75 percent of those went to Ivy League schools!"

A burst of applause filled the room as the proud parents sitting next to their sons congratulated Nolan's efforts. Two of the banner carriers, sixteen-year-olds Knox Overstreet and his friend Charlie Dalton, joined in the applause. They both sported Welton blazers, and, sitting between their parents, they personified the Ivy League image. Knox had short curly hair, an outgoing smile, and an athletic build. Charlie had a handsome, preppy look about him.

"This kind of accomplishment," Dean Nolan continued as Knox and Charlie looked around at their schoolmates, "is the result of fervent dedication to the principles taught here. This is why parents have

3

been sending their sons here and this is why we are the best preparatory school in the United States." Nolan paused for the applause that followed.

"New students," he continued, directing his attention toward the newest boys to join the ranks of Welton Academy, "the key to your success rests on the four pillars. This applies to seventh graders and transfer students alike." Todd Anderson squirmed again in his seat at the mention of transfer students, his face revealing his self-consciousness. "The four pillars are the bywords of this school, and they will become the cornerstones of your lives.

"Welton Society candidate Richard Cameron," Nolan called, and one of the boys who had carried a banner snapped to his feet.

"Yes, sir!" Cameron shouted. His father, sitting beside him, beamed with pride.

"Cameron, what is tradition?"

"Tradition, Mr. Nolan, is the love of school, country, and family. Our tradition at Welton is to be the best!"

"Good, Mr. Cameron.

"Welton Society Candidate George Hopkins. What is Honor?"

Cameron sat stiffly as his father smiled smugly.

"Honor is dignity and the fulfillment of duty!" the boy answered.

"Good, Mr. Hopkins. Honor Society Candidate Knox Overstreet." Knox, who also held a banner, stood.

"Yes, sir."

"What is discipline?" Nolan asked.

"Discipline is respect for parents, teachers, and headmaster. Discipline comes from within."

"Thank you, Mr. Overstreet. Honor candidate Neil Perry."

Knox sat down, smiling. His parents, sitting on either side of him, patted him with encouragement.

Neil Perry rose to his feet. The breast pocket of his Welton blazer was covered with a huge cluster of achievement pins. The sixteen-year-old stood dutifully, staring angrily at Dean Nolan.

"Excellence, Mr. Perry?"

"Excellence is the result of hard work," Perry replied loudly in a rotelike monotone. "Excellence is the key to all success, in school and everywhere." He sat down and stared directly at the dais. Beside him his unsmiling father was stony eyed and silent, not acknowledging his son in the least.

"Gentlemen," Dean Nolan continued, "at Welton you will work harder than you have ever worked in your lives, and your reward will be the success that all of us expect of you.

"Due to the retirement of our beloved English teacher, Mr. Portius, I hope that you will take this opportunity to meet his replacement, Mr. John Keating, himself an honors graduate of this school, who, for the last several years, has been teaching at the highly regarded Chester School in London."

Mr. Keating, who sat with the other members of

the faculty, leaned slightly forward to acknowledge his introduction. In his early thirties, Keating, who had brown hair and brown eyes, was of medium height—an average-looking man. He appeared to be respectable and scholarly, but Neil Perry's father eyed the new English teacher with suspicion.

"To conclude these welcoming ceremonies," Nolan said, "I would like to call to the podium Welton's oldest living graduate, Mr. Alexander Carmichael, Jr., Class of 1886."

The audience rose to a standing ovation as the octogenarian haughtily shunned offers of help from those beside him and made his way to the podium with painstaking slowness. He mumbled a few words that the audience could barely make out, and, with that, the convocation came to an end. The students and their parents filed out of the chapel and onto the chilly campus grounds.

Weathered stone buildings and a tradition of austerity isolated Welton from the world beyond. Like a vicar standing outside of church on Sunday, Dean Nolan watched students and parents say their good-byes.

Charlie Dalton's mother brushed the hair out of his eyes and hugged him tightly. Knox Overstreet's father gave his son an affectionate squeeze as they walked around the campus pointing to its landmarks. Neil Perry's father stood stiffly, adjusting the achievement pins on his son's jacket. Todd

Anderson stood alone, trying to unearth a stone with his shoe. His parents chatted nearby with another couple, paying no heed to their son. Staring at the ground self-consciously, Todd was startled when Dean Nolan approached him and tried to get a look at his name tag.

"Ah, Mr. Anderson. You have some big shoes to fill, young man. Your brother was one of our best."

"Thank you, sir," Todd said faintly.

Nolan moved on, strolling past parents and students, greeting them and smiling all the time. He stopped when he reached Mr. Perry and Neil, and he put his hand on Neil's shoulder.

"We're expecting great things of you, Mr. Perry," the dean said to Neil.

"Thank you, Mr. Nolan."

"He won't disappoint us," the boy's father said to Nolan. "Right, Neil?"

"I'll do my best, sir." Nolan patted Neil's shoulder and moved on. He noticed that many of the younger boys' chins quivered, and tears slipped out as they said good-bye to their parents, perhaps for the first time.

"You're going to love it here," one father said, smiling and waving as he walked quickly away.

"Don't be a baby," another father snapped at his frightened and tearful son.

Slowly the parents filtered out and cars pulled away. The boys had a new home at Welton Academy, isolated in the green but raw woods of Vermont.

"I want to go home!" one boy wailed. An upper-classman patted his back and led him away toward the dorm.

CHAPTER 2

"Walk, gentlemen. Slow down," a teacher with a Scottish brogue called out. The forty members of the junior class hurried down the dormitory staircase while fifteen senior boys tried to crush their way up.

"Yes, sir, Mr. McAllister," one of the juniors called back. "Sorry, sir." McAllister shook his head at the boys who dashed out of the dorm and across the campus.

Once inside the oak-paneled Academy Honor Room, the juniors stood around or sat in the crinkly old leather chairs, waiting for their turns. Several eyes peered up the staircase against the wall that ed to a second-floor door.

Moments later the door opened and five boys filed silently down the stairs. An old gray-haired teacher shuffled to the door.

9

"Overstreet, Perry, Dalton, Anderson, Cameron," Dr. Hager called out. "Come."

The boys filed up the staircase while two boys sitting below watched them intently.

"Who's the new boy, Meeks?" Pitts whispered to his classmate.

"Anderson," Steven Meeks whispered back. Old Hager spotted the conversation.

"Misters Pitts and Meeks. Demerits," he called down dourly. The boys looked down, turning their heads together, and Pitts rolled his eyes.

Dr. Hager was old, but his eyes were sharp as an eagle's. "That's another demerit, Mr. Pitts," he said.

The boys whom Dr. Hager had called followed him into Headmaster Nolan's inner office, passing his secretary and wife, Mrs. Nolan.

They stood in front of a row of chairs facing Dean Nolan, who sat behind his desk, a hunting dog resting at his side.

"Welcome back, boys. Mr. Dalton, how's your father?"

"Doing fine, sir," Charlie said.

"Your family move into that new house yet, Mr. Overstreet?"

"Yes, sir, about a month ago."

"Wonderful," Nolan smiled briefly. "I hear it's beautiful." He patted the dog and gave him a snack while the boys stood awkwardly waiting.

"Mr. Anderson," Nolan said. "Since you're new

10

here let me explain that at Welton I assign extra-curricular activities on the basis of merit and desire.

"These activities are taken every bit as seriously as your class work, right boys?"

"Yes, sir!" the others said in military unison.

"Failure to attend required meetings will result in demerits. Now, Mr. Dalton: the school paper, the Service Club, soccer, rowing. Mr. Overstreet: Welton Society Candidates, the school paper, soccer, Sons of Alumni Club. Mr. Perry: Welton Society Candidates, Chemistry Club, Mathematics Club, school annual, soccer. Mr. Cameron: Welton Society Candidates, Debate Club, rowing, Service Club, Forensics, Honor Council."

"Thank you, sir," Cameron said.

"Mr. Anderson, based on your record at Balin-crest: soccer, Service Club, school annual. Anything else I should know about?"

Todd stood silent. He struggled to say something, but the words just wouldn't come out.

"Speak up, Mr. Anderson," Nolan said.

"I . . . would . . . prefer . . . rowing . . . sir," Todd said, his voice barely audible. Nolan looked at Todd, who started to shake from head to toe.

"Rowing? Did he say rowing? It says here you played soccer at Balincrest?"

Todd tried to speak again. "I . . . did . . . but . . ." he whispered. Beads of sweat broke out on his brow, and he clenched his hands so tightly

11

his knuckles turned white. As the other boys stared at him, Todd fought back tears.

"You'll like soccer here, Anderson. All right, boys. Dismissed."

The boys marched out, Todd's face white with misery. At the door, Dr. Hager called out five more names.

As they headed across campus toward their dorms, Neil Perry approached Todd, who was walking alone, and offered a handshake.

"I hear we're going to be roommates," he said. "I'm Neil Perry."

"Todd Anderson," he replied softly. The boys walked in awkward silence.

"Why'd you leave Balincrest?" Neil asked.

"My brother went here."

Neil shook his head. "Oh, so you're THAT Anderson."

Todd shrugged and groaned. "My parents wanted me to go here all along but my grades weren't good enough. I had to go to Balincrest to pull them up."

"Well, you've won the booby prize," Neil laughed. "Don't expect to like it here."

"I don't already," Todd said.

They walked into the entrance hall of the dorm to find a confusion of students, suitcases, typewriters, pillows, and record players.

At the head of the hall a school porter stood

watching a pile of unclaimed luggage. Neil and Todd stopped to look for their belongings. Neil spotted his bags and went to find their room.

"Home, sweet home," he chuckled as he entered the small square space barely large enough to fit two single beds, two closets, and two desks. He plopped his suitcases on one of the beds.

Richard Cameron stuck his head in the room. "Heard you got the new boy. Hear he's a stiff. Oops!" Cameron said as Todd walked in.

Cameron quickly ducked out. Todd walked past him, dropped his suitcases on the other bed and began to unpack.

"Don't mind Cameron," Neil said. "He's a jerk." Todd just shrugged, focusing on the task at hand.

Knox Overstreet, Charlie Dalton, and Steven Meeks then showed up at their room. "Hey, Perry," Charlie said, "rumor has it you did summer school."

"Yeah, chemistry. My father thought I should get ahead."

"Well," Charlie said. "Meeks aced Latin, and I didn't quite flunk English, so if you want, we've got our study group."

"Sure, but Cameron asked me too. Anybody mind including him?"

"What's his specialty," Charlie laughed, "brown-nosing?"

"Hey," Neil said, "he's your roommate!"

"That's not my fault." Charlie shook his head.

Todd continued unpacking his suitcase while the

other boys talked. Steven Meeks walked toward him.

"Hi, I don't think we've met. I'm Steven Meeks."

Todd extended his hand shyly. "Todd Anderson."

Knox and Charlie walked over and extended their hands in greeting, too.

"Charlie Dalton."

"Knox Overstreet." Todd shook their hands formally.

"Todd's brother is Jeffrey Anderson," Neil said.

Charlie looked over with recognition. "Oh, yeah, sure. Valedictorian, National Merit Scholar . . ."

Todd nodded. "Well, welcome to 'Hellton.'" Meeks laughed.

"It's every bit as hard as they say. Unless you're a genius like Meeks," Charlie said.

"He only flatters me so I'll help him with Latin."

"And English, and trig . . ." Charlie added. Meeks smiled.

There was another knock on the door. "It's open," Neil called. But it wasn't another of their buddies this time.

"Father," Neil stammered, his face turning white. "I thought you'd left!"

CHAPTER 3

The boys jumped to their feet. "Mr. Perry," Meeks, Charlie, and Knox said in unison.

"Keep your seats, boys," Neil's father said as he walked briskly into the room. "How's it going?"

"Fine, sir. Thank you," they answered.

Mr. Perry stood face to face with Neil, who shuffled uncomfortably. "Neil, I've decided that you're taking too many extracurricular activities. I've spoken to Mr. Nolan about it, and he's agreed to let you work on the school annual *next* year," he said, and then walked toward the door.

"But, Father," Neil cried. "I'm the assistant editor!"

"I'm sorry, Neil," Mr. Perry replied stiffly.

"But, Father, it's not fair. I . . ."

Mr. Perry's eyes glared at Neil, who stopped midsentence. Then he opened the door and pointed to Neil to leave the room.

"Fellows, would you excuse us a minute?" he asked politely. Mr. Perry followed Neil, closing the door behind him.

His eyes raging, Mr. Perry hissed at his son. "I will *not* be disputed in public, do you understand me?"

"Father," Neil said lamely, "I wasn't disputing you. I . . ."

"When you've finished medical school and you're on your own, you can do as you please. Until then, you will listen to ME!"

Neil looked at the floor. "Yes, sir. I'm sorry."

"You know what this means to your mother, don't you?" Mr. Perry said.

"Yes, sir." Neil stood silent in front of his father. His resolve always crumbled under the threats of guilt and punishment. "Oh well, you know me," Neil said, filling the pause. "Always taking on too much."

"Good boy. Call us if you need anything." He turned without further comment and walked off. Neil looked after his father, feeling overwhelmed with frustration and anger. Why did he always let his father get to him like that?

He opened the door to his room and walked back in. The boys tried to look as if nothing had happened, each waiting for the other to speak. Finally Charlie broke the silence.

"Why doesn't he ever let you do what you want?" he asked.

16

"And why don't you just tell him off! It couldn't get any worse," Knox added.

Neil wiped his eyes. "Oh, that's rich," he sneered. "Like you tell YOUR parents off, Mr. Future Lawyer and Mr. Future Banker!" The boys studied their shoes as Neil stormed around the room angrily. He ripped the school annual achievement pin from his blazer and hurled it furiously at his desk.

"Wait a minute," Knox said, walking toward Neil. "I don't let my parents walk on me."

"Yeah," Neil laughed. "You just do everything they say! You'll be in daddy's law firm as sure as I'm standing here." He turned to Charlie who was sprawled across Neil's bed. "And you'll be approving loans till you croak!"

"Okay," Charlie admitted. "So I don't like it any more than you do. I'm just saying . . ."

"Then don't tell me how to talk to *my* father when you're the same way," Neil snapped. "All right?"

"All right," Knox sighed. "Jesus, what are you gonna do?"

"What I have to do. Chuck the annual. I have no choice."

"I certainly wouldn't lose any sleep over it," Meeks said cheerfully. "It's just a bunch of people trying to impress Nolan."

Neil slammed his suitcase shut and slumped onto his bed. "What do I care about any of it anyhow?" He slammed his hand into his pillow, lay back

17

silently, and stared with glazed eyes at the ceiling.

The boys sat around glumly, feeling Neil's disappointment and sadness. "I don't know about anyone else," Charlie said, again breaking the silence, "but I could sure use a refresher in Latin. Eight o'clock in my room?"

"Sure," Neil said tonelessly.

"You're welcome to join us, Todd," Charlie offered.

"Yeah," Knox agreed. "Come along."

"Thank you," Todd said.

After the boys left, Neil got up and picked up the achievement pin he had thrown. Todd started to unpack again. He took out a framed photo of his mother and father with their arms affectionately around an older boy who appeared to be Todd's famous brother, Jeffrey. Neil looked at the photo and noticed that Todd was slightly apart from the family group, with them but not really a part of them. Todd then unpacked an engraved leather desk set and laid it out on his desk.

Neil plopped on his bed and leaned against the headboard. "So, what do you think of my father?" he asked blankly.

"I'll take him over mine," Todd said softly, almost to himself.

"What?" Neil asked.

"Nothing."

"Todd, if you're gonna make it around here, you've got to speak up. The meek might inherit the earth, but they don't get into Harvard; know what I mean?" Todd nodded, folding a white button-down oxford cloth shirt. Neil held the achievement pin in his hand as he spoke. "The bastard!" he shouted suddenly, jabbing his thumb with the metal point of the pin and drawing blood.

Todd winced, but Neil just stared at the blood intently. He pulled the pin out and hurled it against the wall.

CHAPTER 4

The first day of class dawned bright and clear. The junior-class boys dashed in and out of the bathroom, dressing in record time. "Those seventh graders look like they're going to make in their pants, they're so nervous," Neil laughed as he splashed his face with cold water.

"I feel the same way," Todd admitted.

"Don't worry, the first day is always rough," Neil said. "But we'll get through. Somehow we always do." The boys finished dressing and raced to the chemistry building. "Shouldn't have slept so late and missed breakfast," Neil said. "My stomach's growling."

"Mine too," Todd said as they slid into the chem lab. Knox, Charlie, Cameron, and Meeks were already in the class along with some other juniors. In the front of the room a balding, bespectacled teacher handed out huge textbooks.

"In addition to the assignments in the text," he said sternly, "you will each pick three lab experiments from the project list and report on one every five weeks. The first twenty problems at the end of Chapter One are due tomorrow."

Charlie Dalton's eyes popped as he stared at the text and listened to the teacher. He shot a disbelieving glance at Knox Overstreet, and both boys shook their heads in dismay.

Todd was the only one among them who didn't seem fazed by either the book or the things the teacher was saying. The teacher's voice droned on, but the boys stopped listening somewhere around the words "the first twenty problems." Finally, the bell rang, and almost everyone from chemistry moved into Mr. McAllister's classroom.

McAllister, probably the only Latin teacher in the history of contemporary education with a Scottish brogue, wasted no time in getting into the subject. He handed out the books and launched in. "We'll begin by declining nouns," he said. "Agricola, agricolae, agricolae, agricolam, agricola . . ." McAllister walked around the room, repeating the Latin words as the boys struggled to keep up with him.

After forty minutes of recitation, McAllister stopped and stood, facing the class. "You will be tested on those nouns tomorrow, gentlemen. You have your work cut out for you." He turned and faced the blackboard as a collective groan rippled across the room. Before McAllister could begin round two, however, they were saved by the bell.

"That guy is nuts! I'll *never* learn all that by tomorrow," Charlie moaned.

"Don't worry," Meeks said. "I'll teach you guys the system. We'll study together tonight. Come on, we're late for math."

Mathematical charts decorated the walls of Dr. Hager's classroom, and books were already waiting for them at their desks.

"Your study of trigonometry requires absolute precision," Dr. Hager instructed. "Anyone failing to turn in a homework assignment will be penalized one point off his final grade. Let me urge you now not to test me on this point. Who would like to begin by defining cosine?"

Richard Cameron stood and recited, "A cosine is the sine of the complement of an angle or arc. If we define an angle A, then . . ."

Dr. Hager bombarded the class with mathematical questions the entire period. Hands flew into the air, students stood up and sat down like robots, reeling off answers, staunchly taking harsh reprimands for mistakes.

The bell rang, but not soon enough. "Thank God," moaned Todd as he piled up his books. "I don't think I could have taken another minute of that."

"You'll get used to old Hager," Meeks consoled him. "Once you get the pace of it, you'll do fine."

"I'm already six paces behind," Todd groaned as the boys walked together to their next class. He didn't say another word as they dragged themselves into the English room, dropped their books on their desks, and fell into the seats.

The new English teacher, wearing a shirt and tie but no jacket, sat at the front of the room, staring out the window. The boys settled down and waited, grateful for a moment to relax and shed some of the pressure of the last few hours. Keating continued to stare out the window. The boys started to shuffle uncomfortably.

Finally Keating stood, picked up a yardstick, and started strolling up and down the aisles. He stopped and stared into the face of one of the boys. "Don't be embarrassed," he said kindly to the blushing boy.

He continued to move around the room, looking intently at the boys as he walked. "Uh-huh," he said aloud, looking at Todd Anderson. "Uh-huh," he repeated, moving toward Neil Perry.

"Ha!" He slapped his free hand with the yardstick and strode forcefully to the front of the room. "Nimble young minds!" Keating shouted, looking around at the class and gesturing with the yardstick.

He jumped dramatically onto his desk and turned to face the class. "'O Captain! My Captain!'" he recited energetically, then looked around the room. "Who knows where that's from? Anybody?

No?" He looked piercingly at the silent boys. No one raised a hand. "It was written, my young scholars," he said patiently, "by a poet named Walt Whitman about Abraham Lincoln. In this class you may refer to me as either Mr. Keating or 'O Captain! My Captain!'"

He jumped down from the desk and resumed strolling the aisles, speaking as he moved. "So that I become the source of as few rumors as possible, let me tell you that, yes, I was a student at this institution many moons ago, and no, at that time I did not possess this charismatic personality.

"However, should you choose to emulate my manner, it can only help your grade. Pick up your textbooks from the back, gentlemen, and let's retire to the Honor Room."

Using the yardstick as a pointer, Keating headed to the door and walked out. The students sat, silent, not sure what to do.

"We'd better go with him," Neil said, leading the class to the back of the room. They each picked up a text, gathered their books, and proceeded to the oak-paneled Welton Honor Room, where they had last waited to see Dean Nolan.

Keating walked around the room as the boys straggled in. He studied the walls, which were lined with class pictures dating back to the 1800s. Trophies of every description filled shelves and glass cases.

Sensing that everyone was seated, Keating

turned toward the class. "Mister"—Keating looked down at his roster—"Pitts," he said. "An unfortunate name. Stand up, Mister Pitts." Pitts stood. "Open your text, Pitts, to page 542 and read for us the first stanza of the poem," Keating instructed.

Pitts leafed through his book. "'To the Virgins, To Make Much of Time'?" he asked.

"That's the one," Keating said, as the boys in the class chuckled out loud.

"Yes, sir," Pitts said. He cleared his throat.

> *"Gather ye rosebuds while ye may,*
> *Old time is still a flying:*
> *And this same flower that smiles today,*
> *Tomorrow will be dying."*

He stopped. "'Gather ye rosebuds while ye may,'" Keating repeated. "The Latin term for that sentiment is *Carpe Diem*. Does anyone know what that means?"

"Carpe Diem," Meeks, the Latin scholar, said. "Seize the day."

"Very good, Mr. . . . ?"

"Meeks."

"Seize the day," Keating repeated. "Why does the poet write these lines?"

"Because he's in a hurry?" one student called out as the others snickered.

"No, No, No! It's because we're food for worms, lads!" Keating shouted. "Because we're only going to experience a limited number of springs, summers, and falls.

"One day, hard as it is to believe, each and every one of us is going to stop breathing, turn cold, and die!" He paused dramatically. "Stand up," he urged the students, "and peruse the faces of the boys who attended this school sixty or seventy years ago. Don't be timid; go look at them."

The boys got up and walked to the class pictures lining the honor-room walls. They looked at faces of young men, staring out at them from the past.

"They're not that different than any of you, are they? Hope in their eyes, just like yours. They believe themselves destined for wonderful things, just like many of you. Well, where are those smiles now, boys? What of the hope?"

The boys stared at the photos, their faces sober and reflective. Keating walked swiftly around the room, pointing from photo to photo.

"Did most of them not wait until it was too late before making their lives into even one iota of what they were capable? In chasing the almighty deity of success, did they not squander their boyhood dreams? Most of those gentlemen are fertilizing daffodils now! However, if you get very close, boys, you can hear them whisper. Go ahead," he urged, "lean in. Go on. Hear it? Can you?" The boys were quiet, some of them leaned hesitantly toward the photographs. "Carpe Diem," Keating whispered loudly. "Seize the day. Make your lives extraordinary."

Todd, Neil, Knox, Charlie, Cameron, Meeks, Pitts, and the other boys all stared into the pictures on the walls, lost in thoughts that were rudely interrupted by the bell.

"Weird," Pitts said as he gathered up his books.

"But different," Neil said thoughtfully.

"Spooky," Knox added, shivering slightly, as he headed out of the room.

"You think he'll test us on that stuff?" Cameron asked, looking confused.

"Oh, come on, Cameron," Charlie laughed, "don't you get anything?"

CHAPTER 5

After lunch the juniors assembled in the gymnasium for the required physical-education class.

"Okay, gentlemen," the gym master shouted, "we're going to make something of those bodies yet. Start running around the gym. Stop after each round and check your pulse. See me if you don't have a pulse."

The boys groaned and began jogging around the huge gym. The master chuckled and walked to the edge, leaning against the wall to observe the runners.

"Hastings, move it. We've got to get some of that gut off of you," he called to one boy. "Check your pulse.

"Nice run, Overstreet," he called out. "Good pacing." Knox smiled and waved as he passed by the teacher.

None of them thought they'd make it through the

class, but by the end of the period they'd surprised themselves.

"I'm going to die!" Pitts gasped, standing in the shower after the class. "That guy should head a military school!"

"Come on, Pitts, it's good for you," Cameron laughed.

"That's easy for you to say," Pitts shouted back. "The guy didn't embarrass you to death." Pitts turned quickly to face the wall as the gym master strolled through the shower room, monitoring the activity.

"How about a study group?" Meeks called out from the shower. "Right after dinner."

"Great! Good by me," several of the boys agreed.

"Pick up the soap, Harrison," the gym master called out. "You there," he pointed at another boy, "hurry and dry off!"

"Sorry Meeks, I can't make it," Knox said. "I have to sign out to have dinner at the Danburrys' house."

"Who are the Danburrys?" Pitts asked.

"Whew! Big alums," Cameron whistled. "How'd you pull that?"

Knox shrugged. "They're friends of my dad. Probably in their nineties or something."

"Listen," Neil laughed. "Anything is better than the mystery meat we get here."

"I'll second that!" Charlie agreed.

The boys finished getting dressed, tossed their gym clothes in their lockers, and headed out. Todd sat silently on the bench, slowly pulling up his sock.

"A penny for your thoughts?" Neil laughed, as he sat down next to Todd.

"Not even worth that much," Todd said, shaking his head.

"Want to come to the study group?" Neil asked.

"Thanks, but . . . I'd better do history," Todd smiled.

"Okay, you can always change your mind," Neil answered. He gathered up his books and headed out of the gym. Todd watched him leave and then stared into space again. He put on his shoes, picked up his own books, and walked slowly back to the dorm.

In the distance Todd saw the fiery-red sun sinking behind the green perimeter of trees that enclosed the sprawling campus. "It's big, but it's so small here," he sighed, looking around.

Inside the dorm, he smiled at several boys in the hall but walked into his room and quickly closed the door. He put his books on the desk, sighed again loudly, and sat down.

"I can't believe all the work I have to do," he said as he flipped through the stack of books. He opened his history book, took out a notebook, and stared at the first clean sheet of paper. Absently, he scribbled SEIZE THE DAY in big, black letters.

"Seize the day?" he questioned aloud. "How?" He sighed again, ripped the page out of the notebook, and threw it into the wastebasket. He turned a page in the history book and started to read.

"Ready, Overstreet?" Dr. Hager asked, as he walked into the Honors Room, where Knox Overstreet was once again studying the pictures of old Welton students.

"Yes, sir. Thank you, sir," he answered as he followed Dr. Hager out to the school "woody" station wagon parked in front of the building. The changing colors of the Vermont autumn were muted by the darkness. "It's beautiful when the colors change, isn't it, Dr. Hager?" Knox asked enthusiastically.

"Colors? Oh, yes," Hager mumbled as he drove the old wagon to the rambling mansion where the distinguished Danburry family lived.

"Thanks for the ride, Dr. Hager," Knox smiled. "The Danburrys said they'll bring me back to campus."

"No later than nine, my boy," the old teacher said solemnly.

"Yes, sir." He turned and walked to the door of the large, white, colonial house and rang the bell. A beautiful girl, maybe a bit older than he was and wearing a short tennis skirt, opened the door.

"Hi," she said, smiling. Her blue eyes glowed softly.

Knox hesitated, speechless with astonishment. "Ah . . . hi," he finally got out.

31

"Are you here to see Chet?" she asked. He stared at her for a moment, unable to keep his eyes from moving up and down her athletic figure. "Chet?" she repeated, laughing. "Are you here to see Chet?"

"Mrs. Danburry?" Knox stammered as a middle-aged woman stuck her head around the girl.

"Knox," Janette Danburry smiled, as the girl moved back toward the huge staircase. "Come in. We've been waiting for you!"

Knox walked in behind Mrs. Danburry, but his eyes followed the girl who raced up the stairs two steps at a time.

Mrs. Danburry walked into a huge wood-paneled library. "Joe," she said to a sharply dressed man who looked about forty. "This is Knox."

Joe stuck out his hand and smiled warmly. "Knox, good to see you. Come in. Joe Danburry."

"Nice to meet you," Knox smiled, trying to keep himself from looking toward the staircase.

"You're the spitting image of your father. How is he?" Joe asked as he offered Knox a glass of soda.

"Great," Knox nodded. "Just did a big case for GM."

"Ah. I know where you're headed—like father, like son, eh?" Joe laughed. "Have you met our daughter, Virginia?"

"Oh, that was your daughter?" Knox asked enthusiastically, pointing toward the staircase.

"Virginia, say hello," Mrs. Danburry instructed

32

as a cute but rather plain fifteen-year-old girl stood up from the floor on the other side of the room. Her books and pages of neatly written notes were strewn across the floor.

"It's Ginny," she said as she turned to Knox. "Hi," she said and smiled shyly.

"Hello," Knox said, glancing briefly at Ginny, before staring again at the staircase where his eyes stayed glued on the slender legs he saw standing there. He heard a giggle come from that direction, and he turned awkwardly back to Ginny.

"Sit down, sit down," Mr. Danburry said, gesturing toward a comfortable leather chair. "Did your father ever tell you about the case we had together?"

"Pardon?" Knox said absently. The girl in the tennis dress was coming down the stairs with a tall athletic-looking young man.

"He didn't tell you what happened?" Mr. Danburry laughed.

"Er, no," Knox said, unable to take his eyes off the girl. The couple stepped into the room as Mr. Danburry started to recall the story.

"We were really stuck," he reminisced. "I was sure I'd lost the biggest case of my life. Then your father came to me and told me he could weasel a settlement—but only if I gave him the entire fee from our client! The son of a gun!" He slapped his knee. "You know what I did?"

"Huh?" Knox said.

"I let him have it!" he roared. "I was so desperate, I let your father take the whole fee!" Knox faked a laugh, trying to keep up with the hysterical laughter of Mr. Danburry, while his eyes kept darting to the couple standing in the doorway.

"Dad, can I take the Buick?" the young man asked.

"What's wrong with your car?" Joe said. "Chet, where are your manners? Knox, this is my son Chet and his girlfriend, Chris Noel. This is Knox Overstreet."

"We sort of met," Knox said, staring at Chris. "Almost."

"Yes." Chris smiled as she answered.

"Hi," Chet said, totally disinterested.

Mrs. Danburry stood. "Excuse me while I check on dinner," she said.

"Come on, Dad, why is this always a big deal?" Chet asked.

"Because I bought you a sports car and suddenly you want my car all the time."

"Chris's mom feels safer when we're in a bigger car. Right, Chris?" Chet shot her a wicked smile, and Chris blushed.

"It's all right, Chet," she said.

"It's *not* all right. Come on, Dad . . ." Joe Danburry walked out of the room, and Chet followed after him, pleading. "Come on, Dad. You're not using the Buick tonight, so why can't I?"

34

While the bickering continued in the hall, Knox, Ginny, and Chris stood awkwardly in the library.

"So, uh, where do you go to school?" Knox asked.

"Ridgeway High," Chris said. "How's Henley Hall, Gin?"

"Okay," Ginny said flatly.

"That's your sister school, isn't it?" Chris said, looking at Knox.

"Sort of."

"Ginny, are you going out for the Henley Hall play?" Chris asked. "They're doing *A Midsummer Night's Dream*," she explained to Knox.

"Maybe," Ginny shrugged.

"So, how did you meet Chet?" Knox asked Chris. Both girls stared at him. "I mean, er . . ." he stammered.

"Chet plays on the Ridgeway football team, and I'm a cheerleader," Chris explained. "He used to go to Welton but he flunked out." She turned to Ginny. "You should do it, Gin, you'd be great."

Ginny looked down shyly as Chet came to the door. "Chris," he smiled. "We got it. Let's go."

"Nice meeting you, Knox." Chris smiled again as she walked out, hand in hand with Chet. "Bye, Gin."

"Nice meeting you, Chris," Knox choked out.

"Might as well sit down until dinner," Ginny suggested. An awkward moment of silence followed. "Chet just wanted the Buick so they can go

parking," she confided with a blush, not being able
to think of anything better to say.

Knox watched through the window as Chris and
Chet got into the Buick and kissed, long and hard.
His heart was pounding with envy.

Two hours later, Knox staggered into the lobby of
the dorm where Neil, Cameron, Meeks, Charlie,
and Pitts were studying math. Pitts and Meeks
worked on assembling a small crystal radio as the
study session progressed. Knox collapsed onto a
couch.

"How was dinner?" Charlie asked. "You look
shell-shocked. What did they serve, Welton Mystery Meat?"

"Terrible," Knox wailed. "Awful! I just met the
most beautiful girl I have ever seen in my life!"

Neil jumped up from the study group and ran
over to the couch. "Are you crazy? What's wrong
with that?"

"She's practically engaged to Chet Danburry,
Mr. Mondo Jocko himself," Knox moaned.

"Too bad," Pitts said.

"Too bad! It's not too bad, it's a tragedy!"
Knox shouted. "Why does she have to be in love
with a jerk?"

"All the good ones go for jerks," Pitts said
matter-of-factly. "You know that. Forget her. Take
out your trig book and figure out problem 12."

"I can't just forget her, Pitts. And I certainly can't
think about math!"

"Sure you can. You're off on a tangent—so you're halfway into trig already!" Meeks laughed loudly.

"Oh, Meeks! That was terrible," Cameron said, shaking his head.

Meeks grinned sheepishly. "I thought it was clever."

Knox stopped pacing and faced his friends. "You really think I should forget her?"

"You have another choice?" Pitts said.

Knox dropped to his knees in front of Pitts as though he were proposing. "Only you, Pittsie," he implored, with an exaggerated sigh. "There's only you!" Pitts pushed him away, and Knox slumped into a chair in the lobby as the boys resumed their math.

"That's it for tonight, guys," Meeks said, breaking up the study group. "Tomorrow will bring more work, fear not."

"Say, what happened to Todd?" Cameron asked as they gathered up their books.

"Said he wanted to do history," Neil said.

"Come on, Knox," Cameron said. "You'll survive this chick. Maybe you'll think of something to win her love. Remember, seize the day!" Knox smiled, got up from the couch, and followed the boys to their rooms.

The following morning John Keating sat in a chair beside his desk. His mood seemed serious and quiet.

"Boys," he said as the class bell rang, "open your Pritchard text to page 21 of the introduction. Mr. Perry"—he gestured toward Neil—"kindly read aloud the first paragraph of the preface entitled 'Understanding Poetry.'"

The boys found the pages in their text, sat upright, and followed as Neil read: "'Understanding Poetry, by Dr. J. Evan Pritchard, Phd. To fully understand poetry, we must first be fluent with its meter, rhyme, and figures of speech, then ask two questions: 1) How artfully has the objective of the poem been rendered and 2) How important is that objective? Question 1 rates the poem's perfection; question 2 rates its importance. Once these questions have been answered, determining the poem's greatness becomes a relatively simple matter. If the poem's score for perfection is plotted on the horizontal of a graph and its importance is plotted on the vertical, then calculating the total area of the poem yields the measure of its greatness. A sonnet by Byron might score high on the vertical but only average on the horizontal. A Shakespearean sonnet, on the other hand, would score high both horizontally and vertically, yielding a massive total area, thereby revealing the poem to be truly great.'"

Keating rose from his seat as Neil read and went to the blackboard. He drew a graph, demonstrating by lines and shading, how the Shakespeare poem would overwhelm the Byron poem.

Neil continued reading. "'As you proceed through the poetry in this book, practice this rating method. As your ability to evaluate poems in this manner grows, so will your enjoyment and understanding of poetry.'"

Neil stopped, and Keating waited a moment to let the lesson sink in. Then Keating grabbed onto his own throat and screamed horribly. "AHHH-HGGGGG!!" he shouted. "Refuse! Garbage! Pus! Rip it out of your books. Go on, rip out the entire page! I want this rubbish in the trash where it belongs!"

He grabbed the trash can and dramatically marched down the aisles, pausing for each boy to deposit the ripped page from his book. The whole class laughed and snickered.

"Make a clean tear," Keating cautioned. "I want nothing left of it! Dr. J. Evans Pritchard, you are disgraceful!" The laughter grew, and it attracted the attention of the Scottish Latin teacher, Mr. McAllister, across the hall. Mr. McAllister came out of his room and peeked into the door window as the boys ripped the pages from their books. Alarmed, he pulled open the door and rushed into Keating's room.

"What the . . ." McAllister said, until he spotted Keating holding the trash can. "Sorry, I didn't think you were here, Mr. Keating." Baffled and embarrassed, he backed out of the room and quietly closed the door.

Keating strutted back to the front of the room, put the trash can on the floor and jumped into it. The boys laughed louder. Fire danced in Keating's eyes. He stomped the trash a few times, then stepped out and kicked the can away.

"This is battle, boys," he cried. "War! You are souls at a critical juncture. Either you will succumb to the will of academic hoi polloi, and the fruit will die on the vine—or you will triumph as individuals.

"Have no fear, you will learn what this school wants you to learn in my class; however, if I do my job properly, you will also learn a great deal more. For example, you will learn to savor language and words because no matter what anyone tells you, words and ideas have the power to change the world. A moment ago I used the term 'hoi polloi.' Who knows what it means? Come on, Overstreet, you twerp."

The class laughed. "Anderson, are you a man or a boil?" The class laughed again, and everyone looked at Todd. He tensed visibly, and, unable to speak, jerkily shook his head. "No."

Meeks raised his hand. "The hoi polloi. Doesn't it mean 'the herd'?"

"Precisely, Meeks," Keating said. "Greek for 'the herd.' However, be warned that when you say 'the hoi polloi,' you are actually saying, 'the the herd,' indicating that you, too, are hoi polloi!"

Keating grinned wryly, and Meeks smiled. The teacher paced to the back of the room. "Now Mr.

Pitts may argue that nineteenth-century literature has nothing to do with business school or medical school. He thinks we should study our J. Evans Pritchard, learn our rhyme and meter, and quietly go about our business of achieving other ambitions."

Pitts smiled and shook his head. "Who, me?" he asked.

Keating slammed his hand on the wall behind him, and the sound reverberated like a drum. The entire class jumped and turned to the rear. "Well," Keating whispered defiantly. "I say—drivel! One reads poetry because he is a member of the human race, and the human race is filled with passion! Medicine, law, banking—these are necessary to sustain life. But poetry, romance, love, beauty? These are what we stay alive for!

"I quote from Whitman:

> "O me! O life! of the questions of
>   these recurring,
> Of the endless trains of the faithless,
>   of cities fill'd with the foolish, . . .
> What good amid these, O me, O life?
>   Answer
> That you are here—That life exists and iden-
>   tity,
> That the powerful play goes on, and you may
>   contribute a verse."

Keating paused. The class sat silent, taking in the message of the poem. Keating looked around again

41

and repeated awestruck, "'That the powerful play goes on, and you may contribute a verse.'"

He stood silent at the back of the room, then slowly walked to the front. All eyes were riveted on his impassioned face. Keating looked around the room. "What will *your* verse be?" he asked intently.

The teacher waited a long moment, then softly broke the mood. "Let's open our texts to page 60 and learn about Wordsworth's notion of romanticism."

CHAPTER 6

McAllister pulled out a chair next to Keating at the teachers' dining table and sat down. "Mind if I join you?" he asked, as he plopped his huge frame into the seat and signaled to a waiter for service.

"My pleasure," Keating smiled. He looked out at the room filled with blazer-clad boys eating lunch.

"Quite an interesting class you had today, Mr. Keating," McAllister said sarcastically.

Keating looked up. "Sorry if I shocked you."

"No need to apologize," McAllister said as he shook his head, his mouth already filled with the mystery meat of the day. "It was quite fascinating, misguided though it was."

Keating raised his eyebrows. "You think so?"

McAllister nodded. "Undeniably. You take a big risk encouraging them to be artists, John. When they realize that they're not Rembrandts or Shakespeares or Mozarts, they'll hate you for it."

"Not artists, George," Keating said. "You missed the point. Free thinkers."

"Ah," McAllister laughed, "free thinkers at seventeen!"

"I hardly pegged you as a cynic," Keating said, sipping a cup of tea.

"Not a cynic, my boy," McAllister said knowingly. "A realist! Show me the heart unfettered by foolish dreams, and I'll show you a happy man!" He chewed a bite. "But I will enjoy listening to your lectures, John," McAllister added. "I'll bet I will."

Keating grinned with amusement. "I hope you're not the only one who feels that way," he said, glancing at several of the boys from the junior class who were seated nearby.

The boys all turned as Neil Perry walked quickly into the dining room and sat down with them.

"You guys won't believe this!" he said, puffing breathlessly. "I found his senior annual in the library." Neil looked toward Keating, who was engaged in animated conversation with Mr. McAllister at the teacher's table. He opened the annual and read: "'Captain of the soccer team, editor of the annual, Cambridge-bound, Man most likely to do anything, Thigh man, Dead Poets Society.'"

The others tried to grab the old annual. "Thigh man?" Charlie laughed, "Mr. K. was a hell-raiser. Good for him!"

"What is the Dead Poets Society?" Knox asked,

as he leafed through the book of old photos of Keating's Welton class.

"Any group pictures in the annual?" Meeks asked.

"Not of that," Neil said, as he studied the captions. "No other mention of it."

Neil looked through the annual as Charlie nudged his leg. "Nolan," he hissed. As the dean approached, Neil passed the book under the table to Cameron, who immediately handed it over to Todd, who looked at him questioningly, then took it.

"Enjoying your classes, Mr. Perry?" Nolan asked as he paused at the boys' table.

"Yes, sir, very much," Neil said.

"And our Mr. Keating? Finding him interesting, boys?"

"Yes, sir," Charlie said. "We were just talking about that, sir."

"Good," Nolan said approvingly. "We're very excited about him. He was a Rhodes scholar, you know." The boys smiled and nodded.

Nolan walked to another table. Todd pulled out the annual from under the table and leafed through it on his lap as he finished lunch

"I'll take the annual back," Neil said to Todd, as they got up to leave the dining room.

"What are you going to do with it?" Todd asked hesitantly.

"A little research," Neil said, smiling smugly.

45

After classes, Neil, Charlie, Meeks, Pitts, Cameron, and Todd headed back to the dorm together. They spotted Mr. Keating, wearing his sport coat and a scarf, walking across the lawn with an arm full of books.

"Mr. Keating?" Neil called after him. "Sir? O Captain! My Captain?" Keating stopped and waited for the boys to catch up with him. "What was the Dead Poets Society, sir?" Neil asked. For a split second, Keating's face reddened. "I was just looking in an old annual," Neil explained, "and . . ."

"Nothing wrong with research," Keating said, regaining his composure.

The boys waited for him to say more. "But what was it?" Neil pressed.

Keating looked around to make sure that no one was watching. "A secret organization," he almost whispered. "I don't know how the present administration would look upon it, but I doubt the reaction would be favorable." His eyes scanned the campus as the boys held their breaths. "Can you boys keep a secret?" They nodded instantly. "The Dead Poets was a society dedicated to sucking the marrow out of life. That phrase is by Thoreau and was invoked at every meeting," he explained. "A small group of us would meet at the old cave, and we would take turns reading Shelley, Thoreau, Whitman, our own verse—and the enchantment of the moment let it work its magic on us." Keating's eyes glowed, recalling the experience.

"You mean it was a bunch of guys sitting around reading poetry?" Knox asked, bewildered.

Keating smiled. "Both sexes participated, Mr. Overstreet. And believe me, we didn't simply read . . . we let it drip from our tongues like honey. Women swooned, spirits soared . . . gods were created, gentlemen."

The boys stood silent for a moment. "What did the name mean?" Neil asked. "Did you only read dead poets?"

"All poetry was acceptable, Mr. Perry. The name simply referred to the fact that, to join the organization, you had to be dead."

"*What?*" the boys said in chorus.

"The living were simply pledges. Full membership required a lifetime of apprenticeship. Alas, even I'm still a lowly initiate," he explained.

The boys looked at one another in amazement. "The last meeting must have been fifteen years ago," Keating recalled. He looked around again to make sure no one was observing, then turned and strode away.

"I say we go tonight," Neil said excitedly when Keating was out of sight. "Everybody in?"

"Where is this cave he's talking about?" Pitts asked.

"Beyond the stream. I think I know where it is," Neil answered.

"That's miles," Pitts complained.

"Sounds boring to me," Cameron said.

"Don't come, then," Charlie shot back.

"You know how many demerits we're talking about here?" Cameron asked Charlie.

"So don't come!" Charlie said. "Please!"

Cameron relented. "All I'm saying is, we have to be careful. We can't get caught."

"Well, no kidding, Sherlock," Charlie retorted sarcastically.

"Who's in?" Neil asked, silencing the argument.

"I'm in," Charlie said first.

"Me too," Cameron added.

Neil looked at Knox, Pitts, and Meeks. Pitts hesitated. "Well . . ."

"Oh, come on, Pitts," Charlie said.

"His grades are hurting, Charlie," Meeks said in Pitts's defense.

"Then you can help him, Meeks," Neil suggested.

"What is this, a midnight study group?" Pitts asked, still unsure.

"Forget it, Pitts," Neil said. "You're coming. Meeks, are your grades hurting, too?" Everyone laughed.

"All right," Meeks said. "I'll try anything *once*."

"Except sex," Charlie laughed. "Right, Meeks, old boy?" Meeks blushed as the boys laughed and horsed around him.

"I'm in as long as we're careful," Cameron said.

"Knox?" Charlie continued.

"I don't know," he said. "I don't get it."

"Come on," Charlie encouraged. "It will help you get Chris."

"It will?" Knox looked mystified. "How do you figure that?"

"Didn't you hear Keating say women swooned!"

"But why?" Knox asked, still uncertain.

The group started to break up, and Knox followed Charlie toward the dorm.

"Why do they swoon, Charlie? Tell me, why do they swoon?" Knox's question remained unanswered when off in the distance a bell rang, summoning the boys to dinner.

After dinner, Neil and Todd went to study hall and sat down at a table together.

"Listen," Neil said to his roommate in a hushed voice. "I'm inviting you to the society meeting." Neil had noticed that no one had asked Todd if he was in. "You can't expect everybody to think of you all the time. Nobody knows you. And you never talk to anyone!"

"Thanks," Todd said, "but it's not a question of that."

"What is it then?" Neil asked.

"I—I just don't want to come," he stammered.

"But why?" Neil asked. "Don't you understand what Keating is saying? Don't you want to do something about it?" Neil quickly turned a page in his book as a study proctor walked by, eyeing the boys suspiciously.

"Yes," Todd whispered, after the proctor was out of earshot. "But . . ."

"But what, Todd? Tell me," Neil begged.

Todd looked down. "I don't want to read."

"What?" Neil looked at him incredulously.

"Keating said everybody took turns reading," Todd said. "I don't want to do it."

"God, you really have a problem, don't you?" Neil shook his head. "How can it hurt you to read? I mean, isn't that what this is all about? Expressing yourself?"

"Neil, I can't explain it." Todd blushed. "I just don't want to do it."

Neil shuffled his papers angrily as he looked at Todd. Then he thought of something. "What if you didn't have to read?" Neil suggested. "What if you just came and listened?"

"That's not the way it works," Todd pointed out. "If I join, the guys will want me to read."

"I know, but what if they said you didn't have to?"

"You mean *ask them*?" Todd's face reddened. "Neil, it's embarrassing."

"No, it's not," Neil said, jumping up from his seat. "Just wait here."

"Neil," Todd called, as the proctor turned and gave him a disapproving look.

Neil was off before Todd could stop him. He slumped miserably in his seat, then opened his history book and began to take notes.

CHAPTER 7

Neil talked in low tones to Charlie and Knox in the dorm hall as the evening parade of prebedtime activity went on around them. Boys moved about the hallway in pajamas, carrying pillows under one arm and books under the other. Neil threw his towel over his shoulder, patted Knox on the back, and headed toward his room. He tossed the towel aside and noticed something on his desk that wasn't there before.

He hesitated momentarily, then picked up an old, well-worn poetry anthology. He opened it and, inside the cover, written in longhand, was the name "J. Keating." Neil read aloud the inscription under the signature. "Dead Poets." He stretched out on his bed and began skimming the thin yellowed pages of the old text. He read for about an hour, vaguely aware of the hallway sounds quieting down, doors slamming shut, and lights being turned off. *There goes Dr. Hager; he's still up,* Neil thought, hearing the resident dorm marshal shuffling up and down the hallway, making sure all was quiet. He seemed to stop right in front of Neil's closed door.

"Quiet," Dr. Hager said aloud, shaking his head. "Too quiet."

Several hours later, certain that everyone was deep in sleep, the boys met at the gnarled old maple tree. They had bundled themselves in winter hats, coats, and gloves, and a few of them had brought flashlights to guide the way. "Gggrrr!" The sound of the school hunting-dog startled them as he sniffed his way out of the bushes.

"Nice doggie," Pitts said, stuffing some cookies in his mouth and leaving a pile of them on the ground. "Let's move it," he hissed as the dog homed in on the food.

"Good thinking, Pittsie," Neil said as the boys crossed the campus under the light of a sky glowing with stars.

"It's cold," Todd complained as they escaped the open, windblown campus and moved through an eerie pine forest, looking for the cave. Charlie ran ahead as the others trudged slowly in the cold.

"We're almost there," Knox said as they reached the bank of the stream and began searching for the cave that was supposed to exist somewhere among the tree roots and brush.

"Yaa! I'm a dead poet!" Charlie shouted, sud-

52

denly popping out of nowhere. He had found the cave.

"Ahh!" Meeks shrieked. "Eat it, Dalton," Meeks said to Charlie, recovering his composure.

"This is it, boys," Charlie smiled. "We're home!"

The boys crowded into the dark cave and spent several minutes gathering sticks and wood, trying to light a fire. The fire came to life and warmed the barren interior. The boys stood silently, as if in a holy sanctuary.

"I hereby reconvene the Welton Chapter of the Dead Poets Society," Neil said solemnly. "These meetings will be conducted by me and by the rest of the new initiates now present. Todd Anderson, because he prefers not to read, will keep minutes of the meetings." Todd winced as Neil spoke, unhappy but unable to speak up for himself.

"I will now read the traditional opening message from society member Henry David Thoreau." Neil opened the book that Keating had left him and read: "'I went to the woods because I wished to live deliberately.'" He skipped through the text. "'I wanted to live deep and suck out all the marrow of life!'"

"I'll second that!" Charlie interrupted.

"'To put to rout all that was not life,'" Neil continued, skipping again. "'And not, when I came to die, discover that I had not lived.'" There was a long silence.

"Pledge Overstreet," Neil said.

53

Knox rose. Neil handed him the book. Knox found another page and read: "'If one advances confidently in the direction of his dreams, he will meet with a success unexpected in common hours.' Yes!" Knox said, his eyes blazing. "I want success with Chris!"

Charlie took the book from Knox. "Come on, man," he said, making a face at Knox, "this is serious." Charlie cleared his throat.

> "There's the wonderful love of a beautiful
>   maid,
> And the love of a staunch, true man,
> And the love of a baby that's unafraid.
> All have existed since time began.
> But the most wonderful love,
> the Love of all loves,
> Even greater than the love for Mother,
> Is the infinite, tenderest, passionate love,
> Of one dead drunk for another."

"Author anonymous," Charlie laughed as he handed the book to Pitts.

"'Here lies my wife: here let her lie. Now she's at rest . . . And so am I!'" Pitts giggled. "John Dryden, 1631–1700. I never thought those guys had a sense of humor!" he said.

Pitts handed the book to Todd while the boys laughed at his joke. Todd froze, holding the book, and Neil quickly took it before the others noticed. Charlie grabbed the book from Neil and read:

> "Teach me to love? Go teach thyself more wit:
> I chief professor am of it.
> The god of love, If such a thing there be,
> May learn to love from me."

The boys "oohhed and aahhed" at Charlie's alleged prowess. "Come on guys, we gotta be serious," Neil said.

Cameron took the book. "This is serious," he said and began to read:

> "We are the music makers
> And we are the dreamers of dreams,
> Wandering by lonely sea-breakers,
> And sitting by desolate streams;
> World losers and world forsakers,
> On whom the pale moon gleams:
> Yet we are the movers and shakers
> Of the world, forever, it seems.
> With wonderful deathless ditties
> We build up with world's great cities,
> And out of a fabulous story
> We fashion an empire's glory:
> One man with a dream, at pleasure
> Shall go forth and conquer a crown;
> And three with a new song's measure

Can trample an empire down.
We in the ages lying,
In the buried past of the earth,
Built Nineveh with our sighing,
And Babel itself with our mirth."

"Amen," several boys uttered.
"Sshh!" hissed the others. Cameron continued:

"And o'erthrew them with prophesying
To the old of the new world's worth;
For each age is a dream that is dying,
Or one that is coming to birth."

Cameron stopped dramatically. "That was by Arthur O'Shaughnessy, 1844–81."

The boys sat quietly. Meeks took the book and leafed through the pages. "Hey, this is great," he said, and started reading seriously:

"Out of the night that covers me,
Black as the Pit from pole to pole
I thank whatever gods may be
For my unconquerable soul!"

"That was W. E. Henley, 1849–1903."
"Come on, Meeks," Pitts scoffed. "You?"
"What?" Meeks said, his look all surprise and innocence.

Knox flipped through the book next and suddenly moaned out loud, reading as though to a vision of Chris in the cave. "'How do I love thee? Let me count the ways. I love thee to the depth . . .'"

Charlie grabbed the book. "Cool it already, Knox," he growled.

The boys laughed. Neil took the book and read to himself for a minute. The boys huddled around the fire that by now was growing dimmer.

"Sshh," Neil said, reading deliberately,

> "Come my friends,
> 'Tis not too late to seek a newer world. . . .
> for my purpose holds
> To sail beyond the sunset . . . and though
> We are not now that strength which in old days
> Moved earth and heaven; that which we are,
>   we are;—
> One equal temper of heroic hearts,
> Made weak by time and fate, but strong in will
> To strive, to seek, to find, and not to yield."

"From 'Ulysses,' by Tennyson," he concluded. The boys grew silent, touched by Neil's impassioned reading and Tennyson's statement of purpose.

Pitts took the book. He started to pound out a congo rhythm as he read the poem:

"Fat black bucks in a wine-barrel room,
Barrel-house kings, with feet unstable,
Sagged and reeled and pounded on the table,
Beat an empty barrel with the handle of a
*   broom,*
Hard as they were able,
Boom, boom, BOOM,
With a silk umbrella and the handle of a
*   broom,*
Boomlay, boomlay, boomlay, BOOM.
THEN I had religion, THEN I had a vision.
I could not turn from their revel in derision.
THEN I SAW THE CONGO, CREEPING
*   THROUGH THE BLACK,*
CUTTING THROUGH THE FOREST WITH
*   A GOLDEN TRACK. . . ."*

As Pitts continued to read, the boys were en-
tranced by the compelling rhythm of the poem.
They danced and clowned to the beat, jumping and
whooping around. Their gestures grew steadily
wilder and more ridiculous and they began to make
jungle noises, beating their legs and heads. Pitts
continued reading as Charlie led the group, dancing and howling, out of the cave and into the night.

They danced wildly in the forest, swaying with
the tall trees and the howling wind.

The fire in the cave went out and the forest
turned pitch black. The boys stopped dancing, and,
as soon as they did, they started to shiver, partly

from the cold and partly from the exhilaration they felt from having let their imaginations run free.

"We'd better get going," Charlie said. "Before you know it, we'll have to be in class."

They snaked through the woods to a clearing that led back to the Welton campus. "Back to reality," Pitts said as they stood facing the campus.

"Or something," Neil sighed. They ran quietly to their dorm, slipped out the twig that held the rear door open, and tiptoed to their rooms.

The next day several of the night revelers yawned as they sat in Mr. Keating's class. Keating, however, paced vigorously back and forth in front of the room.

"A man is not very tired, he is exhausted. Don't use very sad, use . . ." He snapped his fingers and pointed to a boy.

"Morose?"

"Good!" Keating said with a smile. "Language was invented for one reason, boys—" He snapped his fingers again and pointed to Neil.

"To communicate?"

"No," Keating said. "To woo women. And, in that endeavor, laziness will not do. It also won't do in your essays."

The class laughed. Keating closed his book, then walked to the front of the room and raised a map that had covered the blackboard. On the board was a quotation. Keating read it aloud to the class:

*"Creeds and schools in abeyance, I permit
to speak at every hazard, Nature without
check with original energy . . ."*

"Uncle Walt again," he said. "Ah, but the difficulty of ignoring those creeds and schools, condi-
tioned as we are by our parents, our traditions, by
the modern age. How do we, like Walt, permit our
own true natures to speak? How do we strip
ourselves of prejudices, habits, influences? The
answer, my dear lads, is that we must constantly
endeavor to find a new point of view." The boys
listened intently. Then suddenly Keating leaped up
on his desk. "Why do I stand here?" he asked.

"To feel taller?" Charlie suggested.

"I stand on my desk to remind myself that we
must constantly force ourselves to look at things
differently. The world looks different from up here.
If you don't believe it, stand up here and try it. All
of you. Take turns."

Keating jumped off. All of the boys, except for
Todd Anderson, walked to the front of the room,
and, a few at a time, took turns standing on
Keating's desk. Keating strolled up and down the
aisles expectantly as he watched them.

"If you're sure about something," he said as they
slowly returned to their seats, "force yourself to
think about it another way, even if you know it's
wrong or silly. When you read, don't consider only
what the author thinks, but take time to consider
what *you* think.

"You must strive to find your own voice, boys, and the longer you wait to begin, the less likely you are to find it at all. Thoreau said, 'Most men lead lives of quiet desperation.' Why be resigned to that? Risk walking new ground. Now . . ." Keating walked to the door as all eyes followed him intently. He looked at the class, then flashed the room lights on and off over and over again, crying out a noise that sounded like crashing thunder. "In addition to your essays," he said after this boisterous demonstration, "I want each of you to write a poem—something of your own—to be delivered aloud in class. See you Monday."

With that he walked out of the room. The class sat mute and baffled by their eccentric teacher. After a moment, Keating popped his head back in, grinning impishly. "And don't think I don't know this assignment scares you to death, Mr. Anderson, you mole." Keating held out his hand and pretended to send lightning bolts at Todd. The class laughed nervously, somewhat embarrassed for Todd, who forced out a hint of a smile.

School ended early on Friday, and the boys left Keating's class, happy to have an afternoon off.

"Let's go up to the bell tower and work on that crystal radio antenna," Pitts said to Meeks as they walked across campus. "Radio Free America!"

"Sure," Meeks said. They walked past crowds waiting eagerly for the mailboxes to be filled. A group of boys played lacrosse on the green, and in the distance, Mr. Nolan called out orders to the Welton crew team practicing at the lake.

Knox dropped his books into the basket of his bicycle and cruised around the campus. He approached the Welton gates, checked over his shoulder to make sure he had not been seen, and pedaled furiously out the gates, over the countryside, and into Welton village.

Breathing deeply, he looked around for signs of anyone from Welton Academy as he pedaled over to Ridgeway High School. He stopped at a fence, watching as students boarded three parked buses. Uniformed members of the marching band, practicing their drum rolls and scales, hopped on the first bus. Well-padded football players pushed and shoved their way onto the second bus. Boarding the third bus was a bunch of giggling and singing cheerleaders, including Chris Noel.

Knox stood at the fence watching her. He saw her rush up to Chet, who was carrying his football gear, and kiss him on the lips. Chet pulled her to him, and she giggled, then ran and climbed into the cheerleaders' bus.

Knox got on his bike and slowly pedaled back to Welton. Ever since the dinner at the Danburrys', he'd fantasized about seeing Chris Noel again. But not like this—not in a passionate embrace with Chet Danburry. Knox wondered, could he really come up with the words to make Chris swoon over him?

Later that afternoon, Todd sat on his bed, one elbow leaning on a pad of paper. He started to write something, scratched it out, ripped off the page, and threw it in the trash. He covered his face in frustration just as Neil came flying through the door.

Neil dropped his books on his desk, his face flushed with excitement. "I've found it!" he cried.

"Found what?" Todd asked.

"What I want to do! Right now. What's really inside of me." He handed Todd a piece of paper.

"*A Midsummer Night's Dream*," Todd read. "What is it?"

"A play, dummy."

"I know that," Todd visibly winced. "What's it got to do with you?"

"They're putting it on at Henley Hall. See: 'Open Tryouts.'"

"So?" Todd said.

"So I'm gonna act!" Neil shouted, jumping onto his bed. "Ever since I can remember I've wanted to try it. Last summer I even tried to go to summer stock auditions, but of course my father wouldn't let me."

"And now he will?" Todd asked, raising his eyebrow.

"Hell, no, but that's not the point. The point is that for the first time in my whole life I know what I want, and for the first time I'm gonna do it whether my father wants me to or not! Carpe diem, Todd!"

Neil picked up the play and read a couple of lines. He beamed, clenching his fist in the air with joy.

"Neil, how are you gonna be in a play if your father won't let you?" Todd pressed.

"First I gotta get the part; then I'll worry about that."

"Won't he kill you if you don't let him know you're auditioning?"

"As far as I'm concerned," Neil said, "he won't have to know about any of it."

"Come on, you know that's impossible," Todd said.

"Bull! Nothing's impossible," Neil said with a grin.

"Why don't you ask him first? Maybe he'll say yes," Todd suggested.

"That's a laugh," Neil snickered. "If I don't ask, at least I won't be disobeying him."

"But if he said no before, then . . . " Todd began.

"Whose side are you on, anyway? I haven't even gotten the part yet. Can't I even enjoy the idea for a little while?"

"Sorry," Todd said, turning back to his work. Neil sat on his bed and started to read the play.

"By the way, there's a meeting this afternoon," Neil said. "You coming?"

"I guess," Todd said as he grimaced.

Neil put down the play and looked over at his roommate. "None of what Mr. Keating has to say means anything to you, does it?" he asked, incredulous.

"What is that supposed to mean?" Todd was defensive.

"Being in the club means being stirred up by things. You look about as stirred up as a cesspool."

"You want me out? Is that what you're saying?" Todd said angrily.

"No," Neil said softly. "I want you in. But it means you gotta do something. Not just *say* you're in."

Todd turned angrily. "Listen, Neil, I appreciate your interest in me but I'm not like you," he insisted. "When you say things, people pay attention. People follow you. I'm not like that!"

"Why not? Don't you think you could be?" Neil pressed.

"No!" Todd shouted. "Oh, I don't know. I'll probably never know. The point is, there's nothing you can do about it, so butt out, all right? I can take care of myself just fine, all right?"

"Er, no . . . ." Neil said.

"No?" Todd looked astonished. "What do you mean, 'no'?"

Neil shrugged matter-of-factly and repeated, "No. I'm not going to butt out."

Neil opened his play and began to read again.

Todd just sat and stared at him. "Okay," Todd said, defeated. "I'll go."

"Good." Neil smiled and continued reading the play.

CHAPTER 8

The Dead Poets Society met in the cave before soccer practice that afternoon. Charlie, Knox, Meeks, Neil, Cameron, and Pitts walked around the in-ground clubhouse, exploring its nooks and crannies and carving their names in the walls. Todd walked in late, but once they were all assembled, Neil stood and started the meeting.

"'I went to the woods because I wished to live deliberately. I wanted to live deep and suck out all the marrow of life.'"

"God," Knox wailed, "I want to suck all the marrow out of Chris! I'm so in love, I feel like I'm going to die!"

"You know what the dead poets would say," Cameron laughed, "'Gather ye rosebuds while ye may . . .'"

"But she's in love with the moron son of my father's best friend! What would the dead poets say about that?" Knox walked away from the group in despair.

Neil stood up and headed out. "I gotta get to the tryouts," he announced nervously. "Wish me luck."

"Good luck," Meeks, Pitts, and Cameron said in chorus. Todd was silent as he watched Neil go.

"I feel like I've *never* been alive," Charlie said sadly, as he watched Neil go. "For years, I've been risking *nothing.* I have no idea what I am or what I want to do. Neil knows he wants to act. Knox knows he wants Chris."

"Needs Chris? Must have Chris!" Knox groaned.

"Meeks," Charlie said. "You're the brain here. What do the dead poets say about somebody like me?"

"The romantics were passionate experimenters, Charles. They dabbled in many things before settling, if ever," Meeks said.

Cameron made a face. "There aren't too many places to be an experimenter at Welton, Meeks."

Charlie paced as the boys considered Cameron's observation. He stopped and his face lit up. "I hereby declare this the Charles Dalton Cave for Passionate Experimentation." He smiled. "In the future, anyone wishing entry must have permission from me."

"Wait a minute, Charlie," Pitts objected. "This should belong to the club."

"It should, but I found it, and now I claim it.

Carpe cavem, boys. Seize the cave," Charlie countered with a grin.

"Good thing there's only one of you around here, Charles," Meeks said philosophically, while the others looked at each other and shook their heads. The boys had seized the cave, and in it they'd found a home away from Welton, away from parents, teachers, and friends—a place where they could be people they never dreamed they'd be. The Dead Poets Society was alive and thriving and ready to seize the day.

The boys left the cave reluctantly and got back to campus just in time for practice. "Say, look who's the soccer instructor," Pitts said, as they spotted Mr. Keating approaching the field. He was carrying some soccer balls under one arm and a case under the other.

"Okay, boys, who has the roll?" Keating asked.

"I do, sir," a senior student said, handing Keating the class list.

Keating took the three-page roll and examined it. "Answer with, 'Present,' please," he said. "Chapman?"

"Present."

"Perry?" No one answered. "Neil Perry?"

"He had a dental appointment, sir," Charlie said.

"Ummhmm. Watson?" Keating called. No one answered. "Richard Watson absent too, eh?"

"Watson's sick, sir," someone called out.

"Hmm. Sick indeed. I suppose I should give

Watson demerits. But if I give Watson demerits, I will also have to give Perry demerits . . . and I like Perry." He crumpled the class roll and tossed it away. The boys looked on, astonished. "Boys, you don't have to be here if you don't want to. Anyone who wants to play, follow me."

Keating marched off with the balls and the case in hand. Amazed by his capriciousness, most of the boys followed, talking excitedly among themselves.

"Sit down now, boys," Keating instructed when they reached the middle of the field. "Devotees may argue that one game or sport is inherently better than another," he said, pacing. "For me, the most important thing in all sport is the way other human beings can push us to excel. Plato, a gifted man like myself, once said, 'Only the contest made me a poet, a sophist, an orator.' Each person take a slip of paper and line up, single file."

Keating passed out slips of paper to the curious students. Then ran up the field, placing a ball ten feet in front of the boy at the head of the long line. Todd Anderson stood listlessly at the rear as Keating shouted out a series of commands.

"You know what to do . . . now go!" he called, just as George McAllister walked past the soccer field. McAllister stopped, fascinated, as the first boy stepped out and read loudly from his slip of paper: "'Oh to struggle against great odds, to meet enemies undaunted!'" He ran and kicked the ball toward the goal, missing.

70

"It's all right, Johnson, it's the effort that counts," Keating said, as he put down another ball. He opened up his case and took out a portable record player. As the second boy, Knox, stood waiting his turn, Keating put on a record of classical music, blaring it loudly. "Rhythm, boys!" Keating shouted over the strains of the music. "Rhythm is important."

Knox read loudly: "'To be entirely alone with them, to find out how much one can stand!'" Knox ran and kicked the ball, yelling "Chet!" loudly, just before he smashed it with his foot.

Meeks was now at the head of the line. "'To look strife, torture, prison, popular odium face to face!'" he shouted, running and kicking the ball, squarely and with great intent.

Charlie stepped out next. "'To indeed be a god!'" Charlie shouted, kicking the ball through the goal-post with strength and determination.

McAllister shook his head, smiled, and walked away.

The line of players read and kicked until it got dark. "We'll continue next time, boys," Keating said. "Good effort."

Todd Anderson sighed with relief and started jogging back to the dorm. "Don't worry, Mr. Anderson," Keating called after him. "You'll get a turn, too." He felt himself blush, and when he reached the dorm, he slammed the door behind him, then ran into his room and hurled himself on the bed.

71

"Damn," he cried. He sat up, facing the half-composed poem scribbled on the pad that still lay on his bed. He picked up a pencil, added a line, then broke the pencil in anger. He paced around the room, sighed, picked up another pencil and tried to grind out the words.

"I got it!" Todd heard Neil yelling in the hallway. "Hey, everybody, I got the part! I'm going to play Puck." He opened the door to the room and saw Todd sitting there. "Hey, I'm Puck!"

"Puck you! Pipe down," yelled a voice from down the hall.

Charlie and several other boys came wandering into the room. "All right, Neil! Congratulations!" they cheered.

"Thanks, guys. Now go back to your business. I've got work to do." The boys left, and Neil pulled out an old typewriter from under his bed.

"Neil, how are you gonna do this?" Todd asked.

"Ssshh! That's what I'm taking care of now," Neil explained. "They need a letter of permission."

"From you?" Todd asked.

"From my father and Nolan."

"Neil, you're not gonna . . ." Todd started.

"Quiet, I have to think," Neil said. He mumbled lines from the play and giggled to himself as he typed. Todd shook his head in disbelief and tried to concentrate on his poem.

In Mr. Keating's class the following day, Knox Overstreet was the first to read his original poem.

"I see a sweetness in her smile
Bright light shines from her eyes
But life is complete; contentment mine
Just knowing that she—"

Knox stopped. He lowered his paper. "I'm sorry, Mr. Keating. It's stupid." Knox walked back to his seat.

"It's fine, Knox, a good effort," Keating said. "What Knox has done," Keating said as he faced the class, "demonstrates an important point, not only in writing poetry, but in every endeavor. That is, deal with the important things in life—love, beauty, truth, justice."

He paced in front of the class. "And don't limit poetry to the word. Poetry can be found in music, a photograph, in the way a meal is prepared—*anything* with the stuff of revelation in it. It can exist in the most everyday things but it must never, never be *ordinary*. By all means, write about the sky or a girl's smile, but when you do, let your poetry conjure up salvation day, doomsday, any day. I don't care, as long as it enlightens us, thrills us and—if it's inspired—makes us feel a bit immortal."

"O Captain! My Captain," Charlie asked, "is there poetry in math?" Several boys in the class chuckled.

"Absolutely, Mr. Dalton, there is . . . elegance in mathematics. If everyone *wrote* poetry, the planet would starve, for God's sake. But there must be poetry and we must stop to notice it in even the simplest acts of living or we will have wasted much of what life has to offer. Now, who wants to recite next? Come on, I'll get to everyone eventually."

Keating looked around, but no one volunteered. He walked toward Todd and grinned. "Look at Mr. Anderson. In such agony. Step up, lad, and let's put you out of your misery."

The students all eyed Todd. He stood nervously and walked slowly to the front of the class, his face the mask of a condemned man on his way to execution.

"Todd, have you prepared your poem?" Mr. Keating asked.

Todd shook his head.

"Mr. Anderson believes that everything he has inside of him is worthless and embarrassing. Correct, Todd? Isn't that your fear?"

Todd nodded jerkily.

"Then today we will see that what is inside of you is worth a great deal." Keating took long strides to the blackboard and rapidly wrote, "'I SOUND MY BARBARIC YAWP OVER THE ROOFS OF THE WORLD.' Walt Whitman."

He turned to the class. "A yawp, for those of you who don't know, is a loud cry or yell. Todd, I would like you to give us a demonstration of a barbaric yawp."

"A yawp?" Todd repeated, barely audible.

"A barbaric yawp."

Keating paused, then suddenly lunged fiercely toward Todd. "Good God, boy, yell!" he shouted.

"Yawp!" Todd said in a frightened voice.

"Again! Louder!" Keating shouted.

"YAWP!"

"LOUDER!"

"AAAHHHHHHH!"

"All right! Very good, Anderson. There's a barbarian in there after all." Keating clapped, and the class joined in. Red-faced, Todd relaxed a bit.

"Todd, there's a picture of Whitman over the door. What does he remind you of? Quickly, Anderson, don't think about it."

"A madman," Todd said.

"A madman. What kind of madman? Don't think! Answer!"

"A . . . crazy madman!"

"Use your imagination," Keating urged. "First thing that pops to your mind, even if it's gibberish."

"A . . . a sweaty-toothed madman."

"Now there's the poet speaking," Keating cheered. "Close your eyes. Describe what you see. NOW!" he shouted.

"I . . . I close my eyes. His image flicks beside me," Todd said, then hesitated.

"A sweaty-toothed madman," Keating prompted.

"A sweaty-toothed madman . . ."

"Come on!" Keating cried.

"With a stare that pounds my brain," Todd said.

75

"Excellent! Have him act. Give it rhythm!"

"His hands reach out and choke me . . ."

"Yes . . ." Keating urged.

"All the time he mumbles slowly . . ."

"Mumbles what?"

"Truth . . ." Todd shouted. "Truth is like a blanket that always leaves your feet cold!"

A few boys in the class chuckled, and Todd's tortured face grew angry. "To hell with them!" Keating coaxed. "More about the blanket."

Todd opened his eyes and addressed the class in a defiant cadence. "Stretch it, pull it, it will never cover any of us."

"Go on!" Keating said.

"Kick at it, beat at it, it will never be enough . . ."

"Don't stop!" Keating cried.

"From the moment we enter crying," Todd shouted, struggling, but forcing the words out, "to the moment we leave dying, it will cover just your head as you wail and cry and scream!"

Todd stood still for a long time. Keating walked to his side. "There is magic, Mr. Anderson. Don't you forget this."

Neil started applauding. Others joined in. Todd took a deep breath and for the first time he smiled with an air of confidence.

"Thank you, sir," he said, sitting down.

After class, Neil shook Todd's hand. "I knew you

76

could do it," he smiled. "Great job. See you at the cave this afternoon."

"Thanks, Neil," Todd said, still smiling. "I'll see you."

Later that afternoon, Neil carried a battered lampshade through the woods toward the cave.

"Sorry I'm late," he puffed as he hurried in. The other pledges of the Dead Poets Society sat on the floor around Charlie, who was sitting cross-legged and silent before them, his eyes closed. In one hand he held an old saxophone.

"Look at this," Neil said.

"What is it?" Meeks asked.

"Duh-uh, it's a lampshade, Meeks," Pitts said.

Neil took off the lampshade, pulled out the cord and revealed a small painted statue. "It's the god of the cave," Neil smiled broadly.

"Duh-uh, Pitts," Meeks shot back.

Neil placed the statue, which had a stake sticking out of its head, in the ground. He placed a candle in the stake and lit it. The candle illuminated a red-and-blue drummer boy, his face worn from exposure, but noble. Todd, who was obviously relieved from his success of the day, playfully put the lampshade on his own head.

Charlie cleared his throat loudly. The boys turned toward him and settled in. "Gentlemen," he said, "'Poetrusic' by Charles Dalton."

Charles blew a stream of random and blaring

notes on the saxophone, then suddenly stopped. Trance-like, he began to speak: "'Laughing, crying, tumbling, mumbling, gotta do more. Gotta be more . . .'"

He played a few more notes on the saxophone, then, speaking faster than before, continued, "'Chaos screaming, chaos dreaming, crying, flying, gotta be more! Gotta be more!'"

The cave was silent. Then Charlie picked up the instrument and played a simple but breathtaking melody. The skeptical looks on the boys' faces disappeared as Charlie continued playing, lost in the music, and ending with a long and haunting note.

The boys sat silent, letting the beautiful sound wash over them. Neil spoke first.

"Charlie, that was great. Where did you learn to play like that?"

"My parents made me take clarinet, but I hated it," Charlie said, coming back down to earth. "The sax is more sonorous," he said in a mock British accent.

Suddenly Knox stood up, backed away from the group, and wailed out his torment. "God, I can't take it anymore! If I don't have Chris, I'll kill myself!"

"Knox, you gotta calm down," Charlie said.

"No, I've been calm all my life! If I don't *do* something, it's gonna kill me!"

"Where are you going?" Neil called as Knox headed out of the cave.

"I'm calling her," Knox said, running into the woods.

The society meeting ended abruptly and the boys followed Knox back to the campus. Knox might not die of passivity, but there was a good chance he'd die of embarrassment if he called Chris, and the society pledges felt obliged to stand by their fellow poet.

"I've got to do this," Knox said as he picked up the dorm phone. The boys surrounded him protectively as he boldly dialed her telephone number.

"Hello?" Knox heard Chris's voice on the other end of the phone. He panicked and hung up.

"She's gonna hate me! The Danburrys will hate me. My parents will kill me!" He looked around at the others trying to read their faces. No one said a word. "All right, goddamn it, you're right! 'Carpe Diem,' even if it kills me."

He picked up the phone and dialed again. "Hello?" He heard her voice.

"Hello, Chris, this is Knox Overstreet," he said.

"Knox . . . oh yes, Knox. I'm glad you called."

"You are?" He covered the phone and told his friends excitedly, "She's glad I called!"

"I wanted to call you," Chris said. "But I didn't have the number. Chet's parents are going out of town this weekend, so Chet's having a party. Would you like to come?"

"Well, sure!" Knox beamed.

"Chet's parents don't know about it so please keep it quiet. But you can bring someone if you like."

"I'll be there," Knox said excitedly. "The Danburrys'. Friday night. Thank you, Chris."

He hung up the phone, overcome, and let out a loud yelp. "Can you believe it? She was gonna call *me*! She invited me to a party with her!"

"At Chet Danburry's house," Charlie said flatly.

"Yeah."

"Well?" Charlie asked.

"So?" Knox was getting defensive.

"So you really think she means you're going with her?"

"Well, hell no, Charlie, but that's not the point. That's not the point at all!"

"What is the point?" Charlie pressed.

"The point is she was thinking about me!"

"Ah." Charlie shook his head.

"I've only met her once and already she's thinking about me." Knox almost jumped up and down. "Damn it, it's gonna happen. She's going to be mine!"

He raced out of the phone room, his feet barely touching the floor. His friends looked at each other and shook their heads.

"Who knows?" Charlie asked.

"I just hope he doesn't get hurt," Neil said.

CHAPTER 9

Neil pedaled rapidly through the town square on his way to Henley Hall for rehearsals. He cruised past the town hall and a row of shops and continued along the quiet Vermont road until he reached the white brick buildings of Henley Hall. He slid his bike through the gate and parked it in the rack in front of the building. As he entered the auditorium, the director called out to him.

"Hurry up, Neil. We can't do this scene without our Puck."

Neil smiled and dashed to center stage. He grabbed a stick with a jester's head on the end of it from the prop girl and began:

"Yet but three? Come one more:
Two of both kinds makes up four.
Here she comes, curst and sad.—

81

Cupid is a knavish lad,
Thus to make poor females mad."

Puck looked toward the floor where a mad Hermia, played by Ginny Danburry, crawled onto the stage, exhausted and wild-eyed.

The director, a blond teacher in her forties, stopped Ginny as she started her lines and turned toward Neil. "Good, Neil," she complimented. "I really get the feeling your Puck knows he's in charge. Remember that he takes great delight in what he's doing."

Neil nodded and repeated boldly and impishly: "'Cupid is a knavish lad, thus to make poor females mad!'"

"Excellent," the director said with a smile. "Continue, Ginny."

Ginny crawled back onto the stage and started her lines:

"Never so weary, never so in woe,
Bedabbled with the dew, and torn with briers,
I can no further crawl, no further go . . ."

The director gestured and pointed as the students ran through the scene several times.

"See you tomorrow," Neil called when they'd finally finished rehearsals for the day. He walked to the bike rack in the twilight, his eyes flashing and his face flushed from the thrill he got from acting.

He rode back through the sleepy Vermont town to Welton Academy, repeating the lines he had practiced for the past two hours.

Neil approached the Welton gates cautiously, making sure no one was around. He pumped up the hill to the dorm and parked his bike. As he started into the building, he spotted Todd huddled motionless on the stone wall.

"Todd?" he called, walking over to get a better look. Todd sat shivering in the dark without a coat. "What's going on?" Neil asked, staring at his roommate. Todd didn't answer. "Todd, what's the matter?" Neil said, sitting next to him on the wall. "It's freezing out here!"

"It's my birthday," Todd said flatly.

"It is?" Neil said. "Why didn't you tell me? Happy birthday! You get anything?"

Except for his chattering teeth, Todd sat silent and still. He pointed to a box. Neil opened it to find the same monogrammed desk set Todd already had in the room.

"This is your desk set," Neil said. "I don't get it."

"They gave me the exact same thing as last year!" Todd cried. "They didn't even remember!"

"Oh," Neil said in a hushed tone.

"Oh," Todd mocked.

"Well, maybe they thought you'd need another one, a new one," Neil suggested after a long awkward pause. "Maybe they thought . . ."

"Maybe they don't think at all unless it's about

my brother!" Todd said angrily. "His birthday is always a big to-do." He looked at the desk set and laughed. "The stupid thing is, I didn't even like the first one!"

"Look, Todd, you're obviously underestimating the value of this desk set," Neil said flippantly, trying to change the mood.

"What?"

"I mean," Neil said and tried to smile. "This is one special gift! Who would want a football or a baseball bat or a car when they could get a desk set as wonderful as this one!"

"Yeah!" Todd laughed, infected by Neil's humor. "And just look at this ruler!"

They laughed as they both looked at the desk set. By now it was pitch dark and cold. Neil shivered.

"You know what Dad called me when I was growing up? 'Five ninety-eight.' That's what all the chemicals in the human body would be worth if you bottled them raw and sold them. He told me that was all I'd ever be worth unless I worked every day to improve myself. Five ninety-eight."

Neil sighed and shook his head in disbelief. *No wonder Todd is so screwed up*, he thought.

"When I was little," Todd continued, "I thought all parents automatically loved their kids. That's what my teachers told me. That's what I read in the books they gave me. That's what I believed. Well, my parents might have loved my brother, but they did not love me."

Todd stood, took a deep anguished breath, and walked into the dorm. Neil sat motionless on the freezing stone wall, groping for something to say. "Todd . . ." he called lamely, as he ran in after his roommate.

"Hey," Cameron shouted as the boys started into Mr. Keating's room the next afternoon. "There's a note on the board to meet in the courtyard."

"I wonder what Mr. Keating is up to today." Pitts grinned expectantly.

The boys raced down the hall and out the door into the chilly courtyard. Mr. McAllister peered out from his classroom door, shaking his head in annoyance.

"People," Keating said as the boys gathered around him. "A dangerous element of conformity has been seeping into your work. Mister Pitts, Cameron, Overstreet, and Chapman, line up over here please." He pointed to the four boys to stand near him. "On the count of four, I want you to begin walking together around the courtyard. Nothing to think about. No grade here. One, two, three, go!"

The boys began walking. They walked down one side of the courtyard, across the back, up the other side, and across the front, completing the square.

"That's the way," Keating said. "Please continue."

The boys walked around the courtyard again as

85

the rest of the class and the teacher watched. Soon they began to walk in step, a march-like cadence emanating from the pavement. They continued in a one-two-three-four pattern as Keating began to clap to the rhythm.

"There it is . . . Hear it?" he called, clapping louder in time. "One two, one two, one two, one two . . . We're all having fun, in Mr. Keating's class . . . "

Sitting in his empty classroom grading papers, McAllister observed the commotion through the window. The four marchers picked up on their cadence. They lifted their legs high and swung their arms back and forth, keeping the rhythm alive. The class joined in clapping out the beat.

Distracted by the clapping and cheering, Dean Nolan put down his work and peered through the window at the drill-team activity below. Nolan's eyebrows furrowed as he frowned at Keating clapping and shouting to the English class. *What in the world are they doing?* he wondered.

"All right, stop," Mr. Keating called to the marchers. "You may have noticed how at the beginning Misters Overstreet and Pitts seemed to have a different stride than the others—Pitts with his long lurches, Knox with that light little bounce—but soon all were walking in the same cadence. Our encouragement made it even more marked," he pointed out.

"Now, this experiment was not to single out Pitts

or Overstreet. What it demonstrates is how difficult it is for any of us to listen to our own voice or maintain our own beliefs in the presence of others. If any of you think you would have marched differently, then ask yourself why you were clapping. Lads, there is a great need in all of us to be accepted, but you must trust what is unique or different about yourself, even if it is odd or unpopular. As Frost said, "'Two roads diverged in a wood, and I—I took the one less traveled by,/And that has made all the difference.'"

The bell rang, but the boys remained rooted in their spots, watching Keating and absorbing his message. Then Keating saluted the class and walked off.

Nolan moved away from his window as the class dispersed. *What do I do with this one?* he thought. McAllister, chuckling at Keating's antics, returned to grading his papers.

The boys walked from the courtyard to their next class. "We're meeting at the cave after dinner," Cameron said to Neil.

"What time?"

"Seven-thirty."

"I'll pass it along," Neil said as he walked over to Todd.

Later that night, Todd, Neil, Cameron, Pitts, and Meeks sat around a fire in the cave, warming their hands. A thick fog had moved in, and the trees swayed noisily from the gusty wind.

"It's spooky out tonight," Meeks said with a shiver, moving closer to the fire. "Where's Knox?"

"Getting ready for that party," Pitts chuckled.

"What about Charlie? He's the one who insisted on this meeting," Cameron said.

The others shrugged. Neil opened the meeting: "'I went to the woods because I wanted to live deliberately . . . to live deep and suck out all the marrow of life . . .'" Neil stopped short as he listened to a rustle in the woods. They all heard something, and it sure wasn't the wind. Funny, it sounded like a bunch of girls giggling.

"I can't see a thing," a girl's voice echoed into the cave.

"It's just over here," the boys heard Charlie say.

The fire glowed brightly on the faces of the boys surrounding it as Charlie and two older girls came giggling into the cave.

"Hey, guys," Charlie said, holding his arm around the shoulder of a pretty blond, "meet Gloria and . . ." He hesitated and looked at Gloria's friend, a plain girl, with dark hair and green eyes.

"Tina," she said awkwardly, taking a drink from a can of beer.

"Tina and Gloria," Charlie said happily, "this is the pledge class of the Dead Poets Society."

"It's such a strange name!" Gloria laughed. "Won't you tell us what it means?"

"I told you, it's a secret," Charlie said.

"Isn't he precious?" Gloria oozed as she hugged

Charlie affectionately. The boys looked flabber-gasted at these wild, exotic creatures who had entered their cave. They were obviously older, probably around twenty or so, and the boys all wondered the same thing—where had Charlie picked them up?

"Guys," Charlie said, pulling Gloria close to him as the other boys' eyes opened even wider, "I have an announcement. In keeping with the spirit of passionate experimentation of the Dead Poets, I'm giving up the name Charles Dalton. From now on, call me 'Nuwanda.'"

The girls giggled; the boys groaned. "You mean I can't call you Charlie anymore, honey?" Gloria asked, putting her arms around his neck. "What's 'Numama' mean, sugar?"

"It's Nuwanda, and I made it up," Charlie said.

"I'm cold," Gloria said as she squeezed closer to Charlie.

"Let's get some more twigs for the fire," Meeks said.

Charlie shot Meeks a look as he and the other boys left the cave. Charlie walked to one wall, scraped off some mud and wiped it on his face like an Indian brave. He gave Gloria a sexy stare and followed the boys off into the forest to gather some firewood. Tina and Gloria whispered and giggled.

As the society pledges were tramping through the woods, Knox Overstreet bicycled off campus to the Danburry residence. He parked his bike in the bushes on the side of the house, took off his overcoat, and stuffed it in his saddlebag. He straightened his tie, leapt up the steps to the front door, and knocked. Loud music blared from the house, but no one answered the door. He knocked again, then turned the knob and walked in.

Knox found a wild fraternity party in progress. He saw one couple making out on the entrance hall couch. Other couples were on chairs, couches, stairs, or on the floor, oblivious to anyone else around them. Knox stood in the entrance hall, unsure what to do. Just then he spotted Chris, walking out of the kitchen, her hair an uncombed mess.

"Chris!" he called.

"Oh, hi," she said casually. "I'm glad you made it. Did you bring anybody?"

"No," Knox said.

"Ginny Danburry's here. Look for her," Chris said as she started to walk away.

"But, Chris . . ." Knox shouted over the blasting music.

"I gotta find Chet," she called back. "Make yourself at home."

Knox's shoulders slumped as Chris walked briskly away. He climbed over couples sprawled on the floor and dejectedly looked around for Ginny Danburry. *Some party,* he thought.

* * *

Out near the cave at Welton the boys stumbled in darkness, feeling the ground for twigs and logs.

"Charlie . . ." Neil hissed.

"It's Nuwanda."

"Nuwanda," Neil said patiently. "What's going on?"

"Nothing, unless you object to having girls here," Charlie said.

"Well, of course not," Pitts said, bumping into Neil. "Sorry. It's just that . . . you should have warned us."

"I thought I'd be spontaneous," Charlie whispered. "I mean, that's the point of this whole thing, isn't it?"

"Where'd you find them?" Neil asked.

"They were walking along the fence past the soccer field. Said they were curious about the school so I invited them to the meeting," he said matter-of-factly.

"Do they go to Henley Hall?" Cameron asked.

"I don't think they're in school," Charlie said.

"They're townies?!" Cameron nearly choked.

"Sshh, Cameron, what's the matter with you?" Charlie said. "You act like they're your mother or something. You afraid of them?"

"Hell, no. I'm not afraid of them! It's just, if we get caught with them, we're dead."

"Say, boys, what's going on out there?" Gloria called from the cave.

91

"Just gathering wood," Charlie called back. "We're on our way." Turning to Cameron, Charlie whispered, "You just keep your mouth shut, jerk-off, and there's nothing to worry about."

"Watch out who you call a jerk-off, Dalton!"

"Oh, calm down, Cameron," Neil said.

"It's Nuwanda," Charlie snapped back as he headed into the cave. The others followed. Cameron seethed with anger. He watched the boys enter the cave, waited for a minute, then followed.

They threw their twigs and a log they'd found on the fire, and sat around the growing flames. "Wonder how Knox is making out." Pitts laughed.

"Poor guy," Neil sighed. "He's probably in for a big disappointment."

It was a disappointed Knox who wandered through the huge Danburry house and ended up in the butler's pantry. Several kids stood talking while one couple was kissing passionately. Knox tried not to look as the boy's hands kept moving up the girl's skirt, and she kept pushing them away. Knox spotted Ginny Danburry, and they exchanged embarrassed smiles.

"You Mutt Sanders's brother?" a huge line-backer-type guy asked Knox as he mixed a drink.

"No." Knox shook his head.

"Bubba!" the linebacker called to another huge, drunk jock who leaned against the refrigerator. "This guy look like Mutt Sanders?"

"You his brother?" Bubba asked.

"No relation," Knox said. "Never heard of him. Sorry."

"Say, Steve," Bubba said to the linebacker, "where's your manners? Here's Mutt's brother, and you don't offer him a drink? Want some bourbon?"

"Actually I don't . . . " Steve didn't even hear Knox. He pushed a glass into Knox's hand and filled it with bourbon, adding a tiny splash of coke.

Bubba clicked glasses with Knox. "To Mutt," he said.

"To Mutt," Steve, the linebacker, echoed. "To . . . Mutt," Knox agreed. Bubba and Steve drained their glasses in one swallow. Knox followed their lead and burst into a coughing fit. Steve poured everyone more bourbon. Knox felt as if his whole chest was on fire.

"So what's Mutt been up to?" Bubba asked.

"Actually," Knox said, still coughing, "I don't really . . . know Mutt."

"To Mighty Mutt," Bubba said, holding up his glass.

"To Mighty Mutt," Steve echoed.

"Mighty . . . Mutt," Knox coughed as they drained their glasses again. Knox continued to cough, and the linebacker knocked him on the back.

"Take it easy there, bud," he laughed.

"Well, I'd better find Patsy," Bubba hiccupped as

he slapped Knox on the back. "Say hello to Mutt for me."

"Will do," Knox said. He turned to see Ginny smile at him as she wandered out of the pantry.

"Gimme your glass, bud," Steve called, pouring Knox more bourbon. Knox felt his head begin to swim.

The fire blazed inside the cave. The boys and Gloria and Tina sat closely around the woodpile, mesmerized by the dancing flames. The candle on the head of the "cave god" sputtered.

"I heard you guys were weird, but not this weird," Tina said as she looked at the pitted statue. She pulled out a pint of whiskey and offered some to Neil. He took it and sipped, trying to act as if it were natural to take a swig. He handed it back to Tina.

"Go ahead, pass it around," she said. The fire and the warmth of the whiskey gave her plain face a pretty, flushed glow.

The bottle went around the circle. Each of them tried to pretend he liked the bitter taste. Unlike most of the others, Todd managed to keep from coughing as he swallowed the whiskey down.

"Yeah!" Gloria said, impressed by Todd's drinking. "Don't you guys miss having girls here?" she asked.

"Miss it?" Charlie said. "It drives us crazy! That's part of what this club is about. In fact, I'd like to announce that I've published an article in the school paper, in the name of the Dead Poets Society, demanding girls be admitted to Welton, so we can all stop beating off."

"You what?" Neil shouted, standing up. "How did you do that?"

"I'm one of the proofers," Charlie boasted. "I slipped the article in."

"Oh God," Pitts moaned. "It's over now!"

"Why?" Charlie asked. "Nobody knows who we are."

"Don't you think they'll figure out who did it?" Cameron shouted. "Don't you know they'll come to you and demand to know what the Dead Poets Society is? Charlie, you had no right to do something like that!"

"It's Nuwanda, Cameron."

"That's right," Gloria cooed, putting her arm around Charlie. "It's Nuwanda."

"Are we just playing around out here or do we mean what we say? If all we do is come and read a bunch of poems to each other, what the hell are we doing?" Charlie demanded.

"You still shouldn't have done it," Neil said, pacing around the cave. "You don't speak for the club."

"Hey, would you stop worrying about your precious little necks," Charlie said. "If they catch me, I'll tell them I made it up. All your asses are safe.

Look, Gloria and Tina didn't come here to listen to us argue. Are we gonna have a meeting or what?"

"Yeah. How do we know if we want to join if you don't have a meeting?"

Neil raised his eyebrows questioningly at Charlie. "Join?" he asked.

Charlie ignored him and turned to Tina. "'Shall I compare thee to a summer's day? Thou art more lovely and more temperate—'"

Tina melted into warm goo. "Oh, that's so sweet!" she cried, and threw her arms around Charlie. The other boys tried to appear disinterested, as if they weren't really jealous.

"I wrote that for you," Charlie told Tina.

Her eyes popped in delight. "You did?!"

"I'll write one for you, too, Gloria," he said quickly, noticing her face turn red with envy. He closed his eyes. "'She walks in beauty, like the night . . .'"

Charlie opened his eyes after the first few words and stood up from the fire. Trying to cover up his forgetfulness, he walked across the cave. "'She walks in beauty, like the night,'" he repeated. He turned his back, opened a book, and read quickly to himself, while Gloria watched expectantly. He closed it, put the book down, and turned back to Gloria. "'Of cloudless climes and starry skies;/ And all that's best of dark and bright/Meet in her aspect and her eyes.'"

Gloria squealed with delight. "Isn't he wonderful?"

The other boys sat ashen-faced and seething with jealousy over Charlie's escapades. Gloria squeezed Charlie tight.

At that same moment, Knox Overstreet was experiencing some jealousy of his own as he stumbled through the crowded Danburry house. "Boy, were those guys right," he mumbled to himself as he thought of Chris and Chet and remembered his friends' warning not to get his hopes too high over Chris.

The house was dark, illuminated only by the moonlight streaming through the windows. Music by the Drifters played loudly. Couples were intertwined everywhere, making out.

Drink in hand, Knox tripped over a couple on the floor, tipsy from the innumerable bourbons without coke that he had downed with Bubba and Steve.

"Hey!" an angry voice shouted. "Watch where you're going! What'd ya have, too much to drink, buddy?"

CHAPTER 10

"Sorry," Knox whispered, as he fell onto the sofa. He leaned back, clutching his half-full glass, and took a long swig of the bitter bourbon. It seemed to burn less now as it slid down his throat.

He looked around, loosening up from the effect of the booze. To his left was a tangled couple that sounded like a giant panting beast. To his right was another pair who seemed to have sunk right into the sofa. Knox wanted to stand up, but he realized that the couple he had tripped over was now rolled against his shins, pinning him in place. He looked around and almost giggled. *Oh well, I may as well make himself comfortable*, he said to himself. The bodies surrounding him were too busy to notice him anyway.

The music stopped, and the sound of heavy breathing filled the room. *This sounds like an artificial respiration ward*, Knox thought to himself, wishing he too had a partner. He checked on the couple to his right. *I think he's going to chew her lips off*, he thought. He turned to the couple on his left.

"Oh, Chris, you're so beautiful," he heard the boy's voice say.

Oh my God, it's Chris and Chet! Knox thought, his heart beginning to throb. Chris Noel was sitting right next to him on the couch!

The music started up again, and the strains of the Drifters singing "This Magic Moment" filled the room. Knox's head was spinning. Chris and Chet were going at it full force. Knox tried to look away but his eyes were riveted on Chris.

"Chris," Chet groaned, "you're so gorgeous." Chet kissed Chris hard, and she leaned against Knox. In the moonlit room Knox stared at the outline of Chris's face, the nape of her neck, the curves of her breasts. He quickly downed the rest of his drink and forced himself to look away.

Oh my God, help me, he thought as Chris leaned more heavily on him. Knox's face was contorted in agony as he felt himself struggle with temptation. He tried not to look but he knew he was losing his inner battle.

Suddenly, he turned toward Chris again. He melted as his emotions took over. "Carpe breastum," he said to himself, closing his eyes. "Seize the breast!"

"Huh?" Knox heard Chris say to Chet.

"I didn't say anything," Chet said.

The pair continued to kiss while Knox felt his hand, drawn by a powerful magnetic force, reach out and lightly stroke the nape of Chris's neck, then down toward her breast. He dropped his head back and closed his eyes while he slowly caressed Chris.

Thinking that Chet's hands were on her, Chris responded eagerly and Knox started breathing heavily. "Oh, Chet, that feels fabulous," Chris said in the dark.

"It does?" Chet sounded surprised. "What?"

"You know," she said secretively.

Knox pulled his hand away. Chet looked up for a moment and then kissed Chris again. "Don't stop, Chet," Chris moaned.

"Stop what?"

"Chet . . ."

Knox put his hand back on Chris's neck and started rubbing her, gently moving down toward her breast.

"Oh, oh," Chris moaned.

Chet pulled back, trying to figure out what Chris was talking about, but he gave up and started to kiss her again. Chris moaned with pleasure.

Knox leaned his head back on the sofa. His breathing was slow and deep. The sound of the music in the room grew louder. Unable to resist, he rubbed Chris's chest, getting dangerously close to her breast. Chris was breathing hard now, too.

Knox felt himself slip into ecstasy just as his glass fell out of his hand.

Suddenly, Chet's hand grabbed Knox's hand, and a lamp light rudely flicked on. Knox sat face to face with a furious Chet and Chris, who was totally confused.

"What are you doing?" Chet yelled.

"Knox?" Chris shielded her eyes from the sudden light.

"Chet! Chris!" Knox said, pretending to be surprised. "What are you doing here?"

"Why you . . ." Chet screamed. He smashed Knox in the face with his fist, grabbed him by the shirt and, throwing him to the floor, jumped on him. He began swinging at Knox's face, which Knox tried desperately to protect. "You little jerk!" Chet shouted. Chris tried to pull him away.

"Chet, you don't have to hurt him," Chris said. Chet's fist hit Knox over and over again.

"Chet, stop! He didn't mean anything!" Chris cried. She pushed Chet off. Knox rolled over, holding his face. "That's enough," Chris yelled, banging on Chet's chest, trying to get him away.

Chet stood over Knox, who lay limply holding his bloody nose and bruised face. "I'm sorry, Chris, I'm sorry," Knox cried.

"You want some more, you little . . . Huh? Get the hell out of here!"

Chet moved at Knox again, but Chris and some

of the others held him back. Several of the kids led Knox out of the room.

Staggering toward the kitchen, Knox turned and yelled, drunkenly, "Chris, I'm sorry!"

"Next time I see you, you're dead!" Chet screamed.

The Dead Poets Society was still convened, unaware that one of its pledges was in deep trouble.

In the cave the fire burned brightly, casting eerie shadows on the walls. Gloria sat with her arm around Charlie, staring at him in adoration. The bottle of whiskey passed between Tina and the others.

"Hey guys, why don't you show Tina the Dead Poets garden?" Charlie said, nodding toward the cave entrance.

"Garden?" Meeks said, sounding surprised.

"What garden?" Pitts echoed.

Charlie silently motioned with his eyes for Pitts and the others to get lost. Neil caught on and elbowed Pitts, who got the hint.

"Oh, right. That garden. Come on, guys," he said.

"This is so strange!" Tina said, sounding confused. "You guys even have a garden?"

Everyone had left the cave except Meeks, who stood around looking baffled. "What are you guys talking about?" Meeks asked. Charlie stared at him with daggers in his eyes. "Charles, uh, Nuwanda, we don't have a garden," Meeks said.

Neil came back in and pulled Meeks out. "Come on, you idiot!" Neil laughed.

Charlie waited for them to go. He looked at Gloria and smiled. "God, for a smart guy, he's so stupid!"

Gloria stared into Charlie's eyes. Charlie smiled. "I think he's sweet," she said.

"I think you're sweet," Charlie sighed, closing his eyes and leaning in slowly to kiss her. Just as his lips brushed hers, Gloria stood up.

"You know what really excites me about you?" she asked.

Blinking, Charlie looked up. "What?"

"Every guy that I meet wants me for one thing. . . . You're not like that."

"I'm not?"

"No!" she smiled. "Anybody else would have been all over me by now. Make me up some more poetry," she said.

"But . . ." Charlie stammered.

"Please! It's so wonderful to be appreciated for . . . you know . . . what you have inside." Charlie groaned and put his hand over his face. Gloria turned and looked at him. "Nuwanda? Please . . . ?"

"All right! I'm thinking!" He paused for a moment, then recited:

> *"Let me not to the marriage of true minds*
> *Admit impediments. Love is not love*

Which alters when it alteration finds,
Or bends with the remover to remove."

Gloria moaned with satisfaction. "Don't stop!" Charlie continued to recite as Gloria's moans grew louder.

"O, no, it is an ever-fixèd mark
That looks on tempests and is never shaken;
It is the star to every wandering bark,
Whose worth's unknown, although his height
  be taken . . ."

"This is better than *sex* any day," Gloria cried. "This is ROMANCE!"

Charlie's eyes rolled in frustration, but he continued to recite poems well into the night.

The next day, the entire student body was summoned to the Welton Academy Chapel. A buzz droned among the boys as they moved into their seats, passing copies of school newspapers among themselves.

Knox Overstreet sat down trying to hide his bruised and swollen face. Neil, Todd, Pitts, Meeks, Cameron, and especially Charlie wore faces drawn with exhaustion. Pitts stifled a yawn as he handed Charlie a briefcase.

"All set," Pitts whispered. Charlie nodded.

Dean Nolan entered the chapel as the students

quickly put away all the newspapers and stood. Nolan took long strides to the podium and motioned for the boys to sit down. He cleared his throat loudly.

"In this week's issue of WELTON HONORS there appeared an unauthorized and profane article about the need for girls at Welton. Rather than spend my valuable time ferreting out the guilty parties—and let me assure you I will find them—I am asking any and all students who know anything about this article to make themselves known here and now. Whoever the guilty persons are, this is your only chance to avoid expulsion from this school."

Nolan stood silently, waiting for a response. Suddenly, the sound of a telephone ringing broke the heavy silence. Charlie briskly lifted the briefcase into his lap and opened it. Inside was the ringing telephone. The students whispered in hushed astonishment. No one had ever done something this outrageous at Welton! Undaunted, Charlie answered the phone.

"Welton Academy, hello?" he said for all to hear. "Yes, he is, just a moment. Mr. Nolan, it's for you," Charlie said with mock seriousness.

The dean's face turned beet-red. "What?" Nolan screeched.

Charlie held the receiver out to Nolan. "It's God. He said we should have girls at Welton," Charlie

105

said into the phone as a blast of laughter from the students filled the old stone chapel.

The dean did not hesitate to react to the stunt. Before he knew it, Charlie found himself standing in the middle of Nolan's office as the dean paced furiously. "Wipe that smirk off your face," Nolan hissed. "Who else was involved in this?"

"No one, sir," Charlie said. "It was just me. I do the proofing for the paper, so I inserted my article instead of Rob Crane's."

"Mr. Dalton," Nolan said, "if you think you're the first one to try to get thrown out of this school, think again. Others have had similar notions and they have failed just as surely as you will fail. Assume the position."

Charlie obeyed, and Nolan pulled out a huge, old paddle. The paddle had holes drilled in it to speed its progress. Nolan took off his jacket and moved behind Charlie.

"Count aloud, Mr. Dalton," Nolan instructed as he slammed the paddle into Charlie's buttocks.

"One." Nolan swung the paddle again, this time putting more power into it. Charlie winced. "Two."

Nolan delivered, and Charlie counted. By the fourth lick, Charlie's voice was barely audible and his face was contorted with pain.

Mrs. Nolan, the dean's wife and secretary, sat in the outer office trying not to listen as the punishment proceeded. In the adjacent honor room, three students, including Cameron, worked at easels, sketching the moose heads on the wall. They heard the paddle hitting Charlie and were filled with fear and awe. Cameron couldn't draw the moose.

By the seventh lick, tears flowed freely down Charlie's cheeks. "Count!" Nolan shouted.

By the ninth and tenth licks, Charlie choked on the words. Nolan stopped after the tenth lick and walked around to face the boy. "Do you still insist that this was your idea and your idea alone?" he asked.

Charlie choked back the pain. "Yes . . . sir."

"What is this 'Dead Poets Society?' I want names," Nolan shouted.

Feeling faint, Charlie hoarsely replied, "It's only me, Mr. Nolan. I swear. I made it up."

"If I find that there are others, Mr. Dalton, they will be expelled, and you will remain enrolled. Do you understand? Now stand up."

Charlie obeyed. His face was blood-red as he fought back tears of pain and humiliation.

"Welton can forgive, Mr. Dalton, provided you have the courage to admit your mistakes. You will make your apology to the entire school."

Charlie stumbled out of Nolan's office and headed slowly back to the junior dorm. The boys were milling around in their rooms, walking in and out of the hallway, waiting for their friend to return. When they saw Charlie coming, they all dashed into their rooms and pretended to be studying.

Charlie walked down the hallway, moving slowly,

trying not to show his pain. As he neared his room, Neil, Todd, Knox, Pitts, and Meeks approached him.

"What happened?" Neil asked. "Are you all right? Were you kicked out?"

"No," Charlie said, not looking at anyone.

"What happened?" Neil asked again.

"I'm supposed to turn everybody in, apologize to the school, and all will be forgiven," Charlie said. He opened the door and walked into his room.

"What are you going to do?" Neil asked. "Charlie?"

"Damn it, Neil, the name is Nuwanda," Charlie said, as he gave the boys a loaded look and slammed his door shut.

The boys looked at each other. Smiles of admiration broke out in the group. Charlie had not been broken.

Later that afternoon, Nolan walked into one of the Welton classroom buildings and headed down the corridor to Mr. Keating's room. He stopped at the door, knocked, and entered the classroom. Mr. Keating and Mr. McAllister were talking when he walked in.

"Mr. Keating, may I have a word with you?" Nolan said, interrupting the two teachers.

"Excuse me," McAllister said as he scurried out of the room.

Nolan paused and looked around. "This was my first classroom, John, did you know that?" Nolan said, as he walked slowly around the room. "My first desk," he said nostalgically.

"I didn't know you taught," Keating replied.

"English. Way before your time. It was hard giving it up, I'll tell you." He paused, then looked straight at Keating. "I'm hearing rumors, John, of some unorthodox teaching methods in your classroom. I'm not saying they have anything to do with the Dalton boy's outburst, but I don't think I have to warn you that boys his age are very impressionable."

"Your reprimand made quite an impression, I'm sure," Keating said.

Nolan's eyebrows raised for an instant. He let the comment pass. "What was going on in the courtyard the other day?" he asked.

"Courtyard?" Keating repeated.

"Boys marching. Clapping in unison . . ."

"Oh that. That was an exercise to prove a point. About the evils of conformity. I . . ."

"John, the curriculum here is set. It's proven. It works. If *you* question it, what's to prevent them from doing the same?"

"I always thought education was learning to think for yourself," Keating said.

Nolan laughed. "At these boys' ages? Not on your life! Tradition, John! Discipline." He patted Keating on the shoulder patronizingly. "Prepare them for college, and the rest will take care of itself."

Mr. Nolan smiled and left. Keating stood silent,

staring out the window. After a moment, McAllister stuck his head in the door. He had obviously been listening.

"I wouldn't worry about the boys being too conformist if I were you, John," he said.

"Why is that?"

"Well, you yourself graduated from these hallowed halls, did you not?"

"Yes."

"So, if you want to raise a confirmed atheist," McAllister observed, "give him a rigid religious upbringing. Works every time."

Keating stared at McAllister, then suddenly let out a laugh. McAllister smiled, turned, and disappeared down the hall.

Later that night, Keating walked over to the junior-class dorm. The boys were just hurrying out to club meetings and activities. He approached Charlie, who was walking out the door with a group of friends.

"Mr. Keating!" Charlie said, looking surprised.

"That was a ridiculous stunt, Mr. Dalton," Keating said harshly.

"You're siding with Mr. Nolan?" Charlie said in disbelief. "What about Carpe Diem and sucking all the marrow out of life and all that?"

"Sucking out the marrow doesn't mean getting the bone stuck in your throat, Charles. There is a place for daring and a place for caution, and a wise man understands which is called for." Keating said.

"But I thought . . ." Charlie stammered.

"Getting expelled from this school is not an act of wisdom or daring. It's far from perfect but there are still opportunities to be had here."

"Yeah?" Charlie answered angrily. "Like what?"

"Like, if nothing else, the opportunity to attend *my* classes, understand?"

Charlie smiled. "Yes, sir."

Keating turned toward the other Dead Poets pledges, who stood nearby waiting for Charlie. "So keep your heads about you—the lot of you!" he ordered.

"Yes, sir," they said. Keating smiled slightly and left.

The next day the boys sat in Keating's classroom and watched their teacher walk to the board and scrawl the word "COLLEGE" in big bold letters.

"Gentlemen," he said, "today we will consider a skill which is indispensable for getting the most out of college—analyzing books you haven't read." He paused and looked around as the boys laughed.

"College will probably destroy your love for poetry. Hours of boring analysis, dissection, and criticism will see to that. College will also expose you to all manner of literature—much of it transcendent works of magic that you must devour; some of it utter dreck that you must avoid like the plague."

He paced in front of the class as he spoke.

"Suppose you are taking a course entitled, 'Modern Novels.' All semester you have been reading masterpieces such as the touching *Père Goriot* by Balzac and the moving *Fathers and Sons* by Turgenev, but when you receive your assignment for your final paper, you discover that you are to write an essay on the theme of parental love in *The Doubtful Debutante*, a novel—and I use that term generously here—by none other than the professor himself."

Keating looked at the boys with a raised eyebrow and then continued. "After reading the first three pages of the book, you realize that you would rather volunteer for combat than waste your precious earthly time infecting your mind with this sewage, but do you despair? Take an F? Absolutely not. Because you are prepared."

The boys watched and listened intently. Keating continued to pace. "Open *The Doubtful Deb* and learn from the jacket that the book is about Frank, a farm equipment salesman who sacrifices everything to provide his social-climbing daughter, Christine, with the debut she so desperately desires. Begin your essay by disclaiming the need to restate the plot while at the same time regurgitating enough of it to convince the professor that you've read the book.

"Next, shift to something pretentious and familiar. For instance, you might write, 'What is remarkable to note are the similarities between the

112

author's dire picture of parental love and modern Freudian theory. Christine *is* Electra, her father *is* a fallen Oedipus.

"Finally, skip to the obscure and elaborate like this . . ." Keating paused, then read, "'What is most remarkable is the novel's uncanny connection with Hindu Indian philosopher Avesh Rahesh Non. Rahesh Non discussed in painful detail the discarding of parents by children for the three-headed monster of ambition, money, and social success.' Go on to discuss Rahesh Non's theories about what feeds the monster, how to behead it, et cetera, et cetera. End by praising the professor's brilliant writing and consummate courage in introducing *The Doubtful Deb* to you."

Meeks raised his hand. "Captain . . . what if you don't know anything about someone like Rahesh Non?"

"Rahesh Non never existed, Mr. Meeks. You make him, or someone like him, up. No self-important college professor would dare admit ignorance of such an obviously important figure, and you will probably receive a comment like the one I received."

Keating picked up a paper on his desk and read from it to the class: "'Your allusions to Rahesh Non were insightful and well presented. Glad to see that someone besides myself appreciates this great but forgotten Eastern master. A-plus.'"

He dropped the paper back on his desk. "Gentlemen, analyzing dreadful books you haven't read will be on your final exam, so I suggest you practice on your own. Now for some traps of college exams. Take out a blue book and a pencil, boys. This is a pop quiz."

The boys obeyed. Keating passed out tests. He set up a screen in the front of the room, then went to the back of the room and set up a slide projector.

"Big universities are Sodoms and Gomorrahs filled with those delectable beasts we see so little of here: women," he said and smiled. "The level of distraction is dangerously high, but this quiz is designed to prepare you. Let me warn you, this test will count. Begin."

The boys began their tests. Keating lit up the slide projector and put a slide into the machine. He focused on the screen a slide of a beautiful, college-aged girl, leaning over to pick up a pencil. The girl had a remarkable figure, and, bending over as she did, her panties were exposed. The boys glanced up at the screen from their tests. Almost all of them did double takes.

"Concentrate on your tests, boys. You have twenty minutes," Keating said, as he advanced the projector. This time he focused a slide of a beautiful woman in scanty lingerie from a magazine ad. The boys glanced up at the screen, struggling to concentrate. Keating watched their obvious difficulty, amused, as he continued the slide show of beautiful women in revealing and provocative poses, tight blowups of naked female Greek statues—women in a seemingly endless, tantalizing stream. The boys' heads bobbed up and down from the screen to their blue books. On his paper Knox had written "Chris, Chris, Chris," over and over again as he stared numbly at the screen.

CHAPTER 11

The brisk Vermont winter engulfed the campus at Welton. The once colorful foliage of the fall now blanketed the landscape, and fierce winds blew the brittle leaves in torrents.

Todd and Neil, bundled in hooded down jackets and scarves, walked along a path that wound between buildings, the wind howling as Neil rehearsed his lines for *A Midsummer Night's Dream*.

"'Here, villain, drawn and ready. Where art thou?'" Neil called dramatically from memory.

"'I will be with thee straight,'" Todd read from the script.

"'Follow me, then, to plainer ground!'" Neil boomed, over the winds. "God I love this!"

"The play?" Todd asked.

"Yes, and acting!" Neil bubbled. "It's got to be one of the most wonderful things in the world. Most people, if they're lucky, live about half an exciting life. If I could get the parts, I could live dozens of *great* lives!"

He ran and, with a theatrical flourish, leapt onto a stone wall. "'To be or not to be, that is the question!' God, for the first time in my whole life, I feel completely alive! You have to try it," he said to Todd. He jumped down from the wall. "You should come to rehearsals. I know they need people to work the lights and stuff."

"No thanks."

"Lots of girls," Neil pointed out impishly. "The girl who plays Hermia is incredible."

"I'll come to the performance," Todd promised.

"Bluck, bluck, bluck . . . chicken!" Neil teased. "Now where were we?"

"'Yea, art thou there?'" Todd read.

"Put more into it!" Neil urged.

"'YEA, ART THOU THERE?'" Todd bellowed.

"That's it! 'Follow my voice; we'll try no manhood here.'" He bowed and waved to Todd. "Thanks, buddy. See you at dinner," he called, running into the dorm. Todd stood outside watching him, then shook his head and walked off toward the library.

Neil leapt and danced down the hallway, jestering his way past other students who eyed him curiously. He pushed open his door with a flourish and jumped into the room, fencing the air with the jester's stick.

Abruptly, he stopped. Sitting at his desk was his father! Neil's face turned white with shock.

"Father!"

"Neil, you are going to quit this ridiculous play immediately," Mr. Perry barked.

"Father, I . . ."

Mr. Perry jumped to his feet and pounded his hand on the desk. "Don't you *dare* talk back to me!" he shouted. "It's bad enough that you've wasted your time with this absurd acting business. But you deliberately deceived me!" He paced back and forth furiously as Neil stood shaking in his shoes. "How did you expect to get away with this? Answer me!" he yelled. "Who put you up to this? That Mr. Keating?"

"Nobody . . ." Neil stammered. "I thought I'd surprise you. I've gotten all A's and . . ."

"Did you really think I wouldn't find out? 'My niece is in a play with your son,' Mrs. Marks says. 'You must be mistaken,' I say. 'My son isn't in a play.' You made a liar out of me, Neil. Now you will go to rehearsal tomorrow and tell them you are quitting."

"Father, I have one of the main parts," Neil explained. "The performance is tomorrow night. Father, please . . ."

Mr. Perry's face was white with rage. He moved toward Neil, pointing his finger. "I don't care if the world is coming to an *end* tomorrow night, you are through with that play! Is that clear? IS THAT CLEAR?"

118

"Yes, sir." It was all Neil could force himself to say.

Mr. Perry stopped. He stared long and hard at his son. "I've made great sacrifices to get you here, Neil. You will not let me down."

Mr. Perry turned and stalked out. Neil stood still for a long time, then, walking to his desk, he started pounding on it, harder and harder until his fists went numb and tears began rolling down his cheeks.

Later that evening, all of the society pledges sat together in the Welton dining hall, except Neil, who said he had a headache. They appeared to be having difficulty eating, and old Dr. Hager approached their table, eyeing the boys suspiciously.

"Mr. Dalton, what is wrong, son?" he asked. "Are you having trouble with your meal?"

"No, sir," Charlie replied.

Hager watched the boys. "Misters Meeks and Overstreet and Anderson, are you normally left-handed?" Hager asked after a moment.

"No, sir."

"Then why are you eating with your left hands?"

The boys looked at each other. Knox spoke for the group. "We thought it would be good to break old habits, sir," he explained.

"What is wrong with old habits, Mr. Overstreet?"

"They perpetuate mechanical living, sir," Knox maintained. "They limit your mind."

119

"Mr. Overstreet, I suggest you worry less about breaking old habits and more about developing good study habits. Do you understand?" he said firmly.

"Yes, sir."

"That goes for all of you," Hager said, looking at the table of boys. "Now eat with your correct hands."

The boys obeyed. But once he moved away, Charlie switched hands and began eating with his left hand again. One by one, the others followed.

Finally Neil came to the dining room and walked over to their table. He looked solemn and upset. "You okay?" Charlie asked.

"Visit from my father," Neil said.

"Do you have to quit the play?" Todd asked.

"I don't know," Neil said.

"Why don't you talk to Mr. Keating about it," Charlie suggested.

"What good will that do?" Neil asked glumly.

Charlie shrugged. "Maybe he'll have some advice. Maybe he'll even talk to your father."

"Are you kidding?" Neil laughed shortly. "Don't be ridiculous."

In spite of Neil's objections, the boys insisted that Mr. Keating might be able to help Neil solve his problems. After dinner they walked to the teacher's quarters on the second floor of the dorm. Todd, Pitts, and Neil stood outside Keating's door. Charlie knocked.

"This is stupid," Neil protested.

"It's better than doing nothing," Charlie said. He knocked again, but no one came to the door.

"He's not here. Let's go," Neil begged.

Charlie tried the door knob, and the door clicked open. "Let's wait for him," Charlie said as he walked into Keating's room.

"Charlie! Nuwanda!" the others called from the hall. "Get out of there!" But Charlie refused to come out, and after a few minutes of talking and pleading the others gave into their curiosity and entered Keating's room.

The small space was empty and lonely looking. The boys stood around uncomfortably, shifting on their feet. "Nuwanda," Pitts whispered. "We shouldn't be in here!"

Charlie ignored him and got up to look around the room. A small blue suitcase stood on the floor by the door. A few books, some pretty tattered looking, lay on the bed. Charlie walked to the desk and picked up a framed picture of a beautiful girl who looked to be in her twenties. "Whoa, look at her!" he whistled. Lying next to the picture was a half-written letter. Charlie picked up the paper and read: "'My darling Jessica: It's so lonely at times without you . . . bla bla bla. All I can do to put myself at ease is study your beautiful picture or close my eyes and imagine your radiant smile—but my poor imagination is a dim substitute for you. Oh, how I miss you and wish—'"

Charlie kept reading as the other boys heard the door creak open. They backed away from Charlie, who suddenly stopped reading when he saw Keating standing in the doorway.

"Hello! Mr. Keating! Good to see you!" Charlie cried.

Keating walked over to him and calmly took the letter, folded it, and put it in his pocket. "A woman is a cathedral, boys. Worship one at every chance you get," Keating said. He walked to his bureau, opened a drawer and put the letter in. "Anything else you'd care to rifle through, Mr. Dalton?" he asked, looking at Charlie.

"I'm sorry," Charlie apologized. "I, we . . ." Charlie looked around for help. Neil stepped forward.

"O Captain! My Captain, we came here so I could talk to you about something," he explained.

"Okay," Keating said, looking at the group. "All of you?"

"Actually, I'd like to talk to you alone," Neil said, looking back at the boys. Charlie and the others looked relieved to leave.

"I gotta go study," Pitts said. "Yeah," the rest of the boys added. "See you, Mr. Keating."

They all hurried out and closed the door behind them. "Drop by any time," Keating said as they left.

"Thank you, sir," they called back through the closed door.

Pitts punched Charlie in the shoulder. "Damn it, Nuwanda, you idiot!" he said.

"I couldn't stop myself," Charlie shrugged.

Keating couldn't help smiling to himself. Neil paced back and forth, looking around. "Gosh," he said. "They don't give you much room around here, do they?"

"Maybe they don't want worldly things distracting me from my teaching." Mr. Keating smiled wryly.

"Why do you do it?" Neil asked. "I mean, with all this seize-the-day business, I'd have thought you'd be out seeing the world or something."

"Ah, but I am seeing the world, Neil. The new world. Besides, a place like this needs at least one teacher like me." He smiled at his own joke. "Did you come here to talk about my teaching?"

Neil took a deep breath. "My father is making me quit the play at Henley Hall. When I think about Carpe Diem and all that, I feel like I'm in prison! Acting is everything to me, Mr. Keating. It's what I want to do! Of course, I can see my father's point. We're not a rich family like Charlie's. But he's planned the rest of my life for me, and he's never even asked me what I want!"

"Have you told your father what you just told me? About your passion for acting?" Mr. Keating asked.

"Are you kidding? He'd kill me!"

"Then you're playing a part for him, too, aren't

you," Keating observed softly. The teacher watched as Neil paced anxiously. "Neil, I know this seems impossible, but you have to talk to your father and let him know who you really are," Keating said.

"But, I know what he'll say. He'll say that acting is just a whim and that it's frivolous and that I should forget about it. He'll tell me how they're counting on me and to put it out of my mind, 'for my own good.'"

"Well," Keating said, sitting on his bed. "If it's more than a whim, prove it to him. Show him with your passion and commitment that it's what you really want to do. If that doesn't work, at least by then you'll be eighteen and able to do what you want."

"Eighteen! What about the play? The performance is tomorrow night!"

"Talk to him, Neil," Keating urged.

"Isn't there an easier way?" Neil begged.

"Not if you're going to stay true to yourself."

Neil and Keating sat silent for a long time. "Thanks, Mr. Keating," Neil finally said. "I have to decide what to do."

While Neil spoke with Mr. Keating, Charlie, Knox, Pitts, Todd, and Cameron headed out to the cave. Snow was falling, and a soft white blanket seemed to protect the earth from the cold wind that howled through the valley.

The boys scattered around the candle-lit cave, each busy doing his own thing. No one called the meeting to order. Charlie blew sad, melodious notes on his saxophone. Knox sat in one corner, mumbling to himself, as he worked furiously on a love poem to Chris. Todd sat alone writing something too. Cameron studied. Pitts stood at the wall, scratching a quotation from a book into the stone.

Cameron looked at his watch. "Ten minutes to curfew," he reminded them. No one moved.

"What are you writing?" Knox asked Todd.

"I don't know. A poem," Todd said.

"For class?"

"I don't know."

"We're asking for demerits, guys, if we don't beat it out of here. The snow's coming down hard," Cameron said. Charlie ignored Cameron and kept playing the sax. Todd kept writing. Cameron looked around and shrugged. "I'm leaving," he said and walked alone out of the cave.

Knox read his love poem to Chris to himself, then slapped it on the side of his leg. "Damn it! If I could just get Chris to read this poem," he groaned.

"Why don't you read it to her," Pitts suggested. "It worked for Nuwanda."

"She won't even speak to me, Pitts!" Knox cried. "I called her, and she wouldn't even come to the phone."

"Nuwanda recited poetry to Gloria and she jumped all over him . . . right, Nuwanda?"

Charlie stopped playing his sax. He thought a moment. "Absolutely," he agreed and started blowing notes again.

Off in the distance, the curfew bell rang. Charlie finished his melody, put his sax in its case, and moved out of the cave. Todd, Cameron, and Pitts picked up their papers and followed him out into the night. Knox stood in the cave alone, looking at his poem. Then, shoving it back in his book, he blew out the candle and ran out through the woods with desperate determination.

"If it worked for him, it will work for me," he said to himself as he plotted a scheme to get his words to Chris.

The next morning the ground was thickly covered with snow. Knox left the dorm early, bundled against the freezing weather and icy winds. He cleaned the snow off his bike, carried it to a plowed path, and sped away, down the hills of Welton Academy over to Ridgeway High.

He left his bike outside the school and ran frantically into the crowded hallway. Boys and girls bustled about, hanging coats in lockers, getting books, talking and joking around with each other.

Knox hurried down one corridor and stopped to talk to a student. Then he turned and double-timed it up a flight of stairs to the second floor.

"Chris!" Knox spotted her standing in front of her locker, talking with some girlfriends. She quickly gathered her things and turned as Knox ran up to her.

"Knox! What are you doing here?" She pulled him away from her girlfriends into a corner.

"I came to apologize for the other night. I brought you these, and a poem I wrote."

He held out a bouquet of wilted, frostbitten flowers and the poem. Chris looked at them but did not take them. "If Chet sees you, he'll kill you, don't you know that?" she cried.

"I don't care," he said, shaking his head. "I love you, Chris. You deserve better than Chet and I'm it. Please accept these."

"Knox, you're crazy," Chris said as the bell rang and students ran to their classes.

"Please. I acted like a jerk and I know it. Please?" he begged.

Chris looked at the flowers as though she was considering accepting them. "No," she said, shaking her head. "And stop bugging me!" She walked into a classroom and closed the door.

The hallway was clear. Knox stood holding the drooping bouquet and his poem. He hesitated for a moment, then pulled open the door and walked into Chris's classroom.

The students were settling into their seats. Knox pushed past the teacher who was leaning over a desk, helping a student with his homework.

"Knox!" Chris cried. "I don't believe this!"

"All I'm asking you to do is listen," he said, as he

127

unfolded his poem and began to read. The teacher and the class turned and stared at Knox in amazement.

> "The heavens made a girl named Chris,
> With hair and skin of gold
> To touch her would be paradise
> To kiss her—glory untold."

Chris turned red and covered her face with her hands. Her friends sat barely restraining giggles and looking at each other in amazement. Knox continued reading:

> "They made a goddess and called her
> Chris, How? I'll never know.
> But though my soul is far behind,
> My love can only grow."

Knox read on as though he and Chris were the only ones in the room.

> "I see a sweetness in her smile,
> Bright light shines from her eyes
> But life is complete—contentment is mine,
> Just knowing that she's alive."

Knox lowered the paper and looked at Chris, who, utterly embarrassed, peeked out at him through her fingers. Knox put the poem and the flowers on her desk.

"I love you, Chris," he said. Then he turned and walked out of the room.

CHAPTER 12

Knox flew out of Ridgeway High and raced back to Welton as fast as he could, riding against the blinding snow and over the icy roads. Back on campus, his friends were just finishing their class with Mr. Keating. They were huddled around Keating's desk, laughing, when the bell rang.

"That's it, gentlemen," Keating said, snapping his book shut. Several of the boys groaned, wishing they didn't have to move on to Mr. McAllister's Latin class.

"Neil, could I see you a moment?" the teacher called, as the boys gathered their books and headed out the door.

Neil and Keating waited until the others had left. "What did your father say? Did you talk to him?" Keating asked.

"Yeah," Neil lied.

"Really?" Keating said excitedly. "You told your

father what you told me? You let him see your passion for acting?"

"Yeah." Neil felt the lie grow bigger. "He didn't like it one bit, but at least he's letting me stay in the play. Of course, he won't be able to come. He'll be in Chicago on business. But I think he's gonna let me stay with acting. As long as I keep my grades up."

Neil avoided Mr. Keating's eyes. He was so embarrassed by the lie that he didn't even hear what the teacher said to him. He grabbed his books and said he had to run, while Keating stood looking after him, puzzled.

When Knox finally reached campus he ditched his bike near the kitchen at the rear of the main classroom building and raced inside, cold but triumphant. He stopped for a moment to enjoy the warmth and smell of the huge cooking area, and helped himself to a sweet roll that had just come out of the oven. He ran into the corridor just as classes were changing and immediately spotted the gang.

"How'd it go?" Charlie asked. "Did you read it to her?"

"Yep!" Knox grinned, swallowing the last of the sweet roll.

"All right!" Pitts slapped him on the back in congratulations. "What did she say?"

"I don't know," Knox replied.

"What do you mean, you don't know?" Charlie was puzzled.

The boys surrounded Knox before he could escape and ushered him into a classroom, closing the door behind them. "Okay, Knox," Charlie ordered, "start from the beginning."

That night, the boys milled around the dorm lobby waiting to go to Henley Hall with Mr. Keating for the production of *A Midsummer Night's Dream*. Knox slumped on a chair by himself, still bewildered by his encounter with Chris, exhilarated and confused at the same time.

"Where's Nuwanda?" Meeks asked. "If we don't hurry we're going to miss Neil's entrance!"

"He said something about getting red before he left," Pitts said, shaking his head.

"What does *that* mean?" Cameron asked.

"You know Charlie," Pitts laughed, just as Nuwanda scampered down the stairs.

"What's this getting red?" Meeks asked. Charlie checked around. He opened his shirt and revealed a red lightning bolt painted on his chest.

"What's it for?" Todd wanted to know.

"It's an Indian warrior symbol for virility. Makes me feel potent. Like I can drive girls crazy."

"But what if they *see* it, Nuwanda?" Pitts asked. Charlie winked. "So much the better!"

"You are crazy!" Cameron said as the group headed out of the lobby. As they neared the door, they passed Chris, who was just walking in.

Knox nearly fainted. "Chris!" Knox's heart began to beat wildly.

"Knox, why are you doing this to me?" Chris cried.

Knox looked around. "You can't be here!" he said, pushing her into a corner.

Mr. Keating came down the hall, ready to go, and joined the group of boys at the door. "Come on, fellows," he said with a smile, and they left.

"I'll be right there," Knox called after them, and he ushered Chris out of the building into the snowy night.

"If they catch you here, we'll both be in big trouble," Knox said, his teeth chattering from the cold.

"Oh, but it's fine for you to come barging into my school and make a complete fool out of me?" she shouted.

"Sshh, be quiet. Listen. I didn't mean to make a fool of you," he apologized.

"Well, you did! Chet found out, and he's nuts. It took everything I could do to keep him from coming here and killing you. You have to stop this stuff, Knox!"

"But I love you."

"You say that over and over, but you don't even know me!"

In the distance, Keating and the boys, waiting in the school station wagon, honked for Knox. "Go ahead, I'll walk," he yelled, and the car pulled away. "Of course I know you!" Knox said, turning back to Chris. "From the first time I saw you I knew you had a wonderful soul."

"Just like that?" she asked.

"Of course just like that. That's how you always know when it's right."

"And if it so happens that you're wrong? If it just so happens that I couldn't care less about you?"

"Then you wouldn't be here warning me about Chet," Knox pointed out.

Chris thought this over. "Look," she said, "I've got to go. I'm gonna be late for the play."

"Are you going with Chet?"

"With Chet, to a play? Are you kidding?"

"Then let's go together," Knox suggested.

"Knox, you are so infuriating."

"Just give me one chance. If you don't like me after tonight, I'll stay away forever."

"Uh-huh," Chris said with a cynical smile.

"I promise. Dead Poets Honor. Come with me tonight. Then, if you don't want to see me again, I swear I'll bow out."

Chris hesitated. "God, if Chet found out he'd . . ."

"Chet won't know anything," Knox promised. "We'll sit in the back and sneak away as soon as it's over."

"Knox, if you *promise* that this will be the end of it . . ."

"Dead Poets Honor," he said, raising his hand.

"What is that?"

"My word." He crossed his heart with his fingers and looked sincerely at Chris. She sighed as he led her reluctantly off toward Henley Hall.

Knox and Chris entered the high-school auditorium long after Mr. Keating and the other students had taken seats in front. They sat in the back and when his friends spotted him with Chris they shot him gestures of encouragement.

On stage, the performance had begun. Sporting a crown of flowers, Neil made his grand entrance as Puck, and the Dead Poets Society cheered him loudly. Neil scanned the audience with a momentary look of fear. Todd crossed his fingers.

"'How now, spirit! Whither wander you?'" Neil began as Puck.

"'Over hill, over dale, thorough bush, thorough brier . . .'" an actor playing a fairy responded. Mr. Keating glanced at the boys in the audience and gave a thumbs up signal for Neil.

"'Thou speak'st aright;/I am that merry wanderer of the night. / I jest to Oberon, and make him smile, / When I a fat and bean-fed horse beguile, / Neighing in likeness of a filly foal . . .'"

Neil's friends watched him intently as he delivered his lines with skill and ease, enjoying every moment, getting laughs in all the right places. Todd sat mouthing the lines with him as if this might help Neil get through it. But Neil needed no help.

"He's good! He's really good!!" Charlie whispered excitedly to his friends.

The play continued with the characters of Lysander and Hermia. Ginny Danburry played Hermia, dressed in an eye-catching costume of leaves and twigs.

"'One turf shall serve as pillow for us both; / One heart, one bed, two bosoms, and one troth.'"

"'Nay, good Lysander, for my sake, my dear, / Lie further off yet; do not lie so near,'" Ginny replied as Hermia.

Charlie flipped through the program looking for the name of the girl playing Hermia. "Ginny Danburry! She's beautiful!" he sighed as his eyes returned to her leaves and twigs.

"'But, gentle friend, for love and courtesy / Lie further off, in human modesty; / Such separation as may well be said / Becomes a virtuous bachelor and a maid, / So far be distant; and, good night, sweet friend. / Thy love ne'er alter till thy sweet life end!'" Ginny recited.

Charlie sat enraptured by her. As Ginny and Lysander played their scene, Neil stood in the wings looking out. Suddenly, he spotted his father enter the rear of the auditorium and stand at the back. His pulse quickened but his expression remained calm.

On stage, Lysander and Ginny completed their scene. "'Here is my bed. Sleep give thee all his rest!'" Lysander said.

"'With half that wish the wisher's eyes be pressed!'" Hermia returned.

The pair lay down on the stage, and their characters went to sleep. A musical interlude signaled Puck's re-entry to the scene.

Neil moved in the wordless lyrical revelry uninhibited, joyful, magical. The other characters appeared in the slow motion interlude as well. Hermia, glowing brightly, held Charlie spellbound. Mr. Keating, Todd, and the other boys sat awed and delighted by the whole production. Knox missed most of the show because he stared at Chris in complete rapture, and trying hard not to show it, Chris found herself becoming infatuated with Knox as well.

As the musical interlude ended, Neil stood alone on the stage as Puck. He addressed the entire audience but directed his words toward his father, who had remained standing at the rear of the auditorium.

> *"If we shadows have offended,*
> *Think but this, and all is mended,*
> *That you have but slumbered here*
> *While these visions did appear.*
> *And this weak and idle theme,*
> *No more yielding but a dream,*
> *Gentles, do not reprehend;*
> *If you pardon, we will mend.*
> *And as I am an honest Puck,*

If we have unearnèd luck
Now to scape the serpent's tongue,
We will make amends ere long;
Else the Puck a liar call.
So, good night unto you all.
Give me your hands, if we be friends,
And Robin shall restore amends."

The curtain fell on Neil's closing monologue, and the audience burst into enthusiastic applause. The boys had dispelled all doubt of Neil's talent as an actor, and as they rose to a standing ovation, the entire audience followed suit, cheering Neil and the cast through extra curtain calls.

The actors took their bows one by one. Ginny received great applause, and she smiled at Charlie, who applauded and shouted bravos extra loudly. Knox smiled at Chris and stopped clapping to take her hand. Chris did not resist.

When Neil came out and took his bows, his friends cheered wildly. After the applause, the members of the cast came out into the auditorium and mingled with the audience. Several people rushed to the stage to offer their congratulations.

"Family and friends may meet cast members in the lobby, please!" the director called over the microphone.

"Neil!" Todd and the others called. "We'll meet you in the lobby. You were great!"

Onstage, Ginny Danburry was mobbed by well-wishers. Charlie ignored the director's announcement and leapt onto the stage. "You were great!" he heard another boy tell her. He noticed that Lysander had his arm around Ginny.

"Congratulations, Ginny!" Lysander said, hugging her. Undaunted, Charlie pushed his way over to Ginny.

"Bright light shines from your eyes," he said with total sincerity. Ginny saw that he meant it and smiled back. They stared into each other's eyes until finally Lysander smiled awkwardly and moved away.

Backstage, in the boys' dressing room, the jubilant cast carried Neil on their shoulders in praise of his performance. After a moment of celebration, the director entered the dressing room, a worried look on her face.

"Neil," she whispered in a hushed tone. "Your father." Neil hopped off the shoulders of his friends and followed her out, stopping in the wings to put on his coat. He saw his father standing at the back of the auditorium and paused. Neil stepped off the stage, and, taking off the headpiece as he walked, he slowly approached his father.

Charlie spotted Neil. "Neil?" he called. But Neil did not answer. Then Charlie saw Neil join his father, and sensing that something was wrong, he grabbed Ginny's hand and led her off the stage.

Keating and the gang were waiting for Neil in the

lobby. "Hey everybody, this is Chris," Knox said, joining them.

"Whoa, we've heard a lot about *you*!" Meeks said as Knox stared him down. "I mean . . . you know . . . I mean . . ." Meeks stammered.

Suddenly, the door to the lobby burst open, and Mr. Perry led Neil like a prisoner out of the auditorium toward the front door. Charlie and Ginny came out behind them. People in the crowds yelled congratulations at Neil. Stuck behind the throng, Todd tried to reach his friend.

"Neil, that was great! Neil!" Todd shouted.

"We're having a party!" Knox called.

Neil turned around. "It's no use," he said sadly. Mr. Keating reached Neil and took him by the shoulders.

"Neil, you were brilliant!" Keating beamed.

Mr. Perry pushed Keating's hands away. "You! Keep away from him!" Mr. Perry shouted. A stunned silence followed his harsh words. He led Neil outside to his car and pushed him in. Charlie started to follow them outside, but Keating held him back.

"Don't make it any worse than it is," he said sadly.

Mr. Perry started the car and pulled off. Through the car window, Neil looked like a prisoner being taken to his execution.

"Neil!" Todd screamed as the car drove away.

Stunned, the members of the Dead Poets Society

stood silently in the lobby. Charlie walked over to Mr. Keating. "Is it okay if we walk back?" he asked.

"Sure," Keating said, chilled with sympathy, as he watched the "Dead Poets," along with Chris and Ginny, leave the lobby and walk out into the cold, dark night.

CHAPTER 13

Neil's mother sat in the corner of the small, stuffy study, her eyes swollen with tears. Mr. Perry sat rigidly at his desk.

The door opened and Neil walked in, still wearing his Puck costume, his eyes also red from crying. He looked toward his mother and started to speak, but his father quickly interrupted.

"Son, I am trying very hard to understand why you insist on defying us, but whatever the reason, I am not going to let you ruin your life. Tomorrow I am withdrawing you from Welton and enrolling you in Braden Military School. You are going to Harvard and you are going to be a doctor."

Fresh tears welled in Neil's bloodshot eyes. "Father," he pleaded, "that's ten more years. Don't you see, that's a lifetime!"

"You have opportunities I never dreamed of!"

Mr. Perry shouted. "I won't let you squander them." He stalked out of the room.

Neil's mother looked like she wanted to say something, but she remained silent and followed her husband out of the room.

Neil stood alone, completely drained of emotion, trying not to think about the future his father had just laid out for him.

Rather than walking directly back to Welton, the pledges of the Dead Poets Society decided to go to the cave. Todd, Meeks, Pitts, Charlie and Ginny, and Knox and Chris sat huddled around the blazing candle of the cave god for warmth. Charlie held a half-empty glass of wine, and the empty bottle sat on the ground nearby. The boys stared morosely into the flame, aware that it was a symbol of Neil, who had brought it to the cave.

"Knox," Chris said. "I have to go home now. Chet might call."

"It's just for a little while," Knox said, squeezing her hand. "You promised."

"You're so infuriating!" She half-smiled.

"Where's Cameron?" Meeks asked.

Charlie took a sip of wine. "Who knows; who cares?"

Todd suddenly jumped up and pounded the walls with his fists. "Next time I see Neil's father I'm gonna smash him. I don't care what happens to me!"

"Don't be stupid," Pitts said.

Todd paced up and down the cave. Suddenly, Mr. Keating poked his head in, illuminated from behind by the moonlight.

"Mr. Keating!" the boys cried in surprise.

Charlie hid the bottle of wine and the glass. "I thought I'd find you here," Keating said. "Now we mustn't be glum. Neil wouldn't want it that way."

"Why don't we have a meeting in his honor!" Charlie suggested. "Captain, will you lead it?" The other boys seconded the motion.

"Fellows, I don't know . . ." Keating hesitated.

"Come on, Mr. Keating, please . . ." Meeks urged.

Keating looked around at the pleading faces. "Okay, but only a short one," Keating relented. He thought for a moment, then began: "'I went to the woods because I wanted to live deep and suck out all the marrow of life! To put to rout all that was not life. And not, when I came to die, discover that I had not lived.'" He paused. "From Mr. e.e. cummings:

"dive for dreams
or a slogan may topple you
(trees are their roots
and wind is wind)
trust your heart
if the seas catch fire
(and live by love

though the stars walk backward)
honour the past
but welcome the future
(and dance your death
away at this wedding)
never mind a world
with its villains or heroes
(for god likes girls
and tomorrow and the earth)"

Keating paused and looked around. "Now, who else wants to read?" No one spoke. "Come on boys, don't be shy," he urged.

"I have something," Todd said.

"The thing you've been writing?" Charlie asked. Todd nodded. "Yeah."

The boys were really surprised that Todd had volunteered. He stepped forward and took some crumpled papers from his pocket, passing slips of paper to each of the others.

"Everybody read this between verses," he said, holding up the slips of paper.

Todd opened his poem and read:

"We are dreaming of tomorrow, and tomorrow
*   isn't coming;*
we are dreaming of a glory that we
don't really want.
We are dreaming of a new day when the new
*   day's here already.*

We are running from the battle when it's one
  that must be
fought."

Todd nodded. Everyone read, "And still we
sleep." Todd continued:

"We are listening for the calling but
never really heeding,
Hoping for the future when the future's only
  plans.
Dreaming of the wisdom that we are
dodging daily,
Praying for a savior when salvation's
  in our hands.

"And still we sleep.

"And still we sleep.
And still we pray.
And still we fear . . ."

He paused sadly, "'And still we sleep.'" He
folded up the poem. Everyone in the cave applauded.

"That was great!" Meeks cheered. Todd beamed,
modestly taking in all the praise and the congratu-
latory slaps on the back. Keating smiled with great
pride at his student's enormous progress. He
plucked a spherical icicle hanging from the roof of
the cave and peered into it.

"I hold in my hand a crystal ball. In it I see great things for Todd Anderson," he intoned. Todd faced Mr. Keating, then suddenly, powerfully, they hugged. When they drew apart, Keating turned to the others.

"And now," Keating continued, "'General William Booth Enters Into Heaven,' by Vachel Lindsay. When I pause, you ask, 'Are you washed in the blood of the Lamb?'"

Keating recited: "'Booth led boldly with his big bass drum. . . .'" The others answered, "'Are you washed in the blood of the lamb?'" Keating headed out of the cave, followed by the boys and girls, reciting poetry all the way home.

As his friends paid him homage in the cave, Neil sat alone in his darkened room at home, gazing out the window. The passion had dried up and left his body. All feeling was drained from his face and limbs. He believed he was a brittle empty shell that would soon be crushed by the weight of the falling snow.

CHAPTER 14

The moon was full. The stars were out in abundance. The night was clear and cold. The trees hung heavy with icicles as the boys, Ginny, and Chris followed Mr. Keating out into the night. The freeze had turned the barren forest into a world of sparkling diamonds. The group walked through the woods behind Keating as he recited: "'The Saints smiled gravely and they said, "He's come . . ."'"

"'Are you washed in the blood of the Lamb?'" they chorused.

"'Walking lepers followed rank on rank, lurching bravos from the ditches dank, drabs from the alleyways and drug fiends pale,/Minds still passion ridden, soul-powers frail . . .'"

"'Are you washed in the blood of the Lamb?'" they repeated.

As the Society marched through the still of the night, an ominous silence settled over the Perry home. Mr. and Mrs. Perry got into bed and turned off their bedroom light. They did not hear the door to another room open. Neil walked into the hall. He turned a corner and slipped quietly downstairs.

Moonlight illuminated Mr. Perry's study. Neil walked to his father's desk, opened the top drawer and reached way in the back. He pulled out a key and with it, he unlocked the bottom drawer of the desk. Neil sat in the leather desk chair and, reaching across the desk, he picked up the crown of flowers he'd worn as Puck and put it on his head.

The group stopped beside the waterfall, which had frozen. The icy sculpture seemed to defy the laws of gravity as the students looked at its remarkable form. The sky was incredibly clear. Moonlight bouncing off the snow cast a strange bluish glow on the group as Keating continued the poem:

> "Christ came gently with a robe and crown,
> For Booth the soldier, while the throng knelt
>   down.
> He saw King Jesus. They were face to face,
> and he knelt a-weeping in that holy place."

"'Are you washed in the blood of the Lamb?'" they recited again.

The moonlight and the mystical wonder of the frozen waterfall combined with the magical poetry to set the group dancing and playing in the snow.

They worked themselves into a joyful, frantic revelry.

Knox and Chris drifted away from the group and embraced. They kissed, soft and warm, under the frozen moon.

Mr. and Mrs. Perry were fast asleep when the quick, short sound broke the night's silence. "What was that?" Mr. Perry sat up.

"What?" his wife asked, half-asleep.

"That sound? Didn't you hear it?"

"What sound?"

Mr. Perry climbed out of bed and walked into the hallway. He walked up and down the hall, finally entering Neil's room. He ran out and down the stairs as Mrs. Perry followed, trying to get her robe on over her flailing arms.

Mr. Perry walked into the study and turned on the light. He looked around. Everything seemed normal, but just as he turned to leave, he spotted the glistening black object lying on the carpet—his revolver. Panicked, he moved around the desk until he saw the pale white hand. He gasped.

Neil lay on the floor, bathed in his own blood. Mr. Perry knelt down and embraced his son while his wife let out an anguished scream.

"No!" Mr. Perry cried. "No!"

Mr. Keating and the boys took the girls home and returned to Welton in the early-morning hours.

"I'm wiped, drained," Todd said as he headed to his room. "I'm going to sleep until noon."

But early the next morning, Charlie, Knox, and Meeks walked into Todd's room. The boys' faces were ashen. They looked down at Todd, who snored peacefully.

"Todd, Todd," Charlie called softly.

Todd opened his eyes and sat up, looking exhausted. After a few moments, his eyes adjusted to the light. He closed them and lay back down. Then, feeling for his clock, he picked it up and squinted.

"It's only eight. I gotta sleep," he said, pulling the covers over his head. He sat up suddenly, his eyes wide open. His friends were still standing there, silent, and he sensed that something was wrong.

"Todd, Neil's dead. He shot himself," Charlie said.

Todd felt his head spin. "Oh, my God! Oh, Neil!" he wailed as he jumped from his bed and ran down the hall, screaming, to the bathroom. He sat on his knees in the stall and vomited until he thought his guts would come out. His friends waited helplessly outside.

Todd came out of the stall, wiping his mouth. Tears streamed down his face. He walked back and forth in the bathroom. "Someone has to know it was his father! Neil wouldn't kill himself! He loved living!" he cried.

"You don't seriously think his father . . ." Knox said.

"Not with the gun!" Todd shouted. "Damn it, even if the bastard didn't pull the trigger, he . . ." Todd's sobs drowned his words until, finally, he controlled himself. "Even if Mr. Perry didn't shoot him," Todd said calmly, "he killed him. They have to know that!" He ran across the room, screaming painfully, "Neil! Neil!" Falling against the wall, he started sobbing again, and the boys left him alone, sitting on the floor, to cry out his grief.

Not knowing that the boys even knew, Mr. Keating sat at his desk in his empty classroom, struggling to control his emotion. He stood and walked slowly to Neil's desk. He picked up a book, his own battered and worn poetry anthology, and, as he opened it, his eyes focused on his own writing: "Dead Poets." He slumped heavily into Neil's chair, unable to hold back a cry of anguish and grief.

The following morning was cold and somber, a bleak winter's day with bitter gusts of wind that whipped around the procession led by the haunting lament of the school bagpiper.

Neil was buried in the town of Welton. The Dead Poets carried his coffin on their shoulders. His mother, veiled in black, watched the procession with his father, both of them stunned by their grief.

Mr. Nolan, Mr. Keating, and other teachers and students watched solemnly as Neil was laid to rest.

After the burial, the entire school assembled in the Welton chapel. The teachers, including Mr. Keating, stood along the walls. The assembly sang a hymn before the chaplain spoke.

"Almighty God, grant us the grace to entrust Neil Perry into the arms of thy never-failing mercy. Bless Neil and keep him. Cause the light of your countenance to shine upon him and be gracious unto him. Lift up your eyes upon him and grant him peace, now, and forevermore. Amen."

"Amen."

Mr. Nolan followed the chaplain at the podium.

"Gentlemen, the death of Neil Perry is a tragedy. He was a fine student, one of Welton's best, and he will be missed. We have contacted each of your parents to explain the situation. Naturally, all are quite concerned. At the request of Neil's family, I intend to conduct a thorough inquiry into this matter. Your complete cooperation is expected," Nolan said.

The assembly was dismissed, and the boys filed silently out of the chapel. Charlie, Todd, Knox, Pitts, Meeks, and Cameron walked out together, then went their separate ways.

Later, all but Cameron and Meeks reassembled in the junk-filled trunk room in the basement of their dorm. There was a knock at the door. Meeks entered.

"I can't find him," Meeks shook his head.

"You told him about this meeting?" Charlie asked.

"Twice," Meeks said.

"That's it. Great!" Charlie threw up his hands. He went to the window and looked out across the lawn toward the administration building. He turned and faced his friends. "That's it, guys, we're all fried."

"What do you mean?" Pitts asked.

"Cameron's a fink! He's in Nolan's office right now, finking!"

"About what?". Pitts asked.

"The club, Pitts. Think about it." Pitts and the others looked bewildered. "They need a scape-goat," Charlie said. "Schools go under because of things like this."

The boys sat in the trunk room and stared at each other. Soon they heard the sound of a door opening down the hall. Knox went to the door and looked out to see Cameron entering the hallway. Knox stepped out and motioned for Cameron to hurry up.

"Cameron!" he whispered loudly. Cameron looked at Knox. He hesitated, then walked down the hall and entered the trunk room. The rest of the group stared at him.

"What's going on, guys?" Cameron asked inno-cently.

"You finked, didn't you, Cameron?" Charlie said, grabbing his shirt collar.

Cameron pulled away. "To hell with you, dumbo, I don't know what you're talking about!"

"You just told Nolan everything about the club is what I'm talking about," Charlie shouted.

"In case you hadn't heard, Dalton, there's something called an honor code at this school. If a teacher asks you something, you tell the truth or you're expelled."

Charlie moved toward Cameron again. "Why you . . ."

Meeks and Knox pulled Charlie off. "Charlie . . ." Knox said.

"He's a rat! He's in it up to his eyes so he ratted to save himself!" Charlie shouted.

"Don't touch him, Charlie," Knox warned. "You do and you're out."

"I'm out anyway," Charlie said, pushing back.

"He's right, there. And if you're smart, every one of you will do exactly what I did and cooperate. They're not after us. We're the victims. Us and Neil."

"What does that mean?" Charlie asked. "Who are they after?"

"Why, Mr. Keating, of course. The 'Captain' himself. You didn't really think he could avoid responsibility, did you?"

"Mr. Keating? Responsible for Neil? Is that what

they're saying?" Charlie pulled himself free of Meeks and Knox.

"Who else do you think, dumbo?" Cameron said. "The administration? Mr. Perry? Keating put us up to all this, didn't he? If it wasn't for him, Neil would be cozied up in his room right now, studying his chemistry and dreaming of being called doctor."

"That's not true!" Todd cried. "Mr. Keating didn't tell Neil what to do. Neil loved acting."

"Believe what you want," Cameron shrugged. "But I say let Keating fry. Why ruin our lives?"

"You bastard!" Charlie bolted across the room and struck Cameron in the jaw. Cameron fell to the floor, and Charlie straddled him.

"Charlie!" Knox groaned.

Cameron looked up and grinned as he rubbed his cheek. "You just signed your expulsion papers, Nuwanda," he laughed. He covered his bleeding nose. Charlie turned and walked out. The others followed him.

Cameron lay alone on the floor. He shouted after them, "If you guys are smart, you'll do exactly what I did! They know everything anyway. You can't save Keating, but you can save yourselves!"

CHAPTER 15

In the room, Neil's bed stood stripped and his desk empty. Todd sat at the window, looking across the campus at the administration building. As he watched, he saw Meeks escorted out of the building and toward the dorm by Dr. Hager.

Todd peeked out of the door of the room. Meeks and Hager entered the hallway, and Hager waited while Meeks walked silently back to his room.

He passed Todd without even looking at him, and Todd saw the tears streaming down his face. Meeks slammed his door shut behind him.

"Knox Overstreet," Dr. Hager called, as he waited impatiently at the end of the hall.

Knox came out of his room and joined Hager. They walked out the door and back across the campus.

Todd waited a few minutes, then walked across

the hall to Meeks's room. He knocked. "Meeks, it's Todd," he called.

"Go away," Meeks said, his voice hoarse and throaty. "I have to study."

Todd paused, realizing what had happened. "What happened to Nuwanda?" Todd asked Meeks through the closed door.

"Expelled," Meeks said flatly.

Todd stood stunned. "What did you tell them?" Todd asked, again through the door.

"Nothing they didn't already know," Meeks said.

Todd turned away. He returned to his window and watched as Knox was escorted back to the dorm. Again, Todd peered into the hall. Knox and Hager entered. Knox's chin quivered, on the verge of breaking down, and he went into his room, quietly closing the door. Todd stepped back into his room and leaned against the wall. He was shaken as he realized that Knox had been broken. Then he heard his own name called.

"Todd Anderson." It was Dr. Hager. He waited at the end of the hallway. Todd took a deep breath and looked up at the ceiling. He opened the door and walked slowly toward the teacher.

Dr. Hager shuffled across the campus, huffing and puffing from the obvious strain of all the running back and forth. He stopped outside the administration building, caught his breath, and walked in.

Todd followed Hager up the staircase leading to

158

Mr. Nolan's office, feeling like a man climbing to the gallows.

Nolan sat at his desk, and Todd was startled to see his parents seated nearby.

"Dad, Mom," he said.

"Have a seat, Mr. Anderson," Nolan ordered.

Todd sat in the empty chair that had been placed in front of Nolan's desk. He looked at his parents, who sat steely-eyed and grim. A drop of perspiration fell from his brow and stained his shirt.

"Mr. Anderson, I think we've pretty well put together what's happened here. You do admit to being a part of this Dead Poets Society?" Nolan asked.

Todd looked at his parents and at Nolan. He closed his eyes. Before he could nod "yes," his father spoke.

"Answer him!" Mr. Anderson said angrily.

"Yes," Todd said faintly.

"I can't hear you, Todd," Nolan said.

"Yes, sir," Todd answered, not much louder than before.

Nolan looked at Todd and his parents. He held up a piece of paper. "I have here a detailed description of what went on at your meetings. It describes how your teacher, Mr. Keating, encouraged you boys to organize the club and use it as a source of inspiration for reckless, self-indulgent behavior. It describes how Mr. Keating, both in and out of the classroom, encouraged Neil Perry to follow this obsession of acting when he knew it went directly against the explicit orders of Neil's parents. It is Mr. Keating's blatant abuse of his position as a teacher that led directly to Neil Perry's death."

Nolan handed the paper to Todd. "Read this carefully, Todd," Nolan added. "If you don't have anything to add or amend, sign it."

Todd took the paper and read it, spending a long time doing so. By the time he finished, his hands and the paper were shaking. He looked up. "What . . . what is going . . . to . . . happen . . . to Mr. Keating?" he asked Nolan.

His father stood up and shook his fist. "What does that have to do with you?"

"It's all right, Mr. Anderson," Nolan said. "Sit down please. I want him to know." He turned to Todd. "We are not yet clear as to whether Mr. Keating has broken any laws. If he has, he will be prosecuted. What we can do—and yours and the other signatures will help to guarantee it—is see to it that Mr. Keating will never teach again."

"Never . . . teach . . . ?" Todd stammered.

His father stood again and moved toward Todd. "I've had enough," he shouted. "Sign the paper, Todd."

"Please, darling," his mother said from her seat. "For our sakes."

"But . . . teaching is his life! It means everything to him!" Todd cried.

"What do you care?" Mr. Anderson shouted.

"What do you care about me?" Todd shouted back. "He cares about me! You don't!"

Todd's father stood over him, white with rage, and picked up the pen. "Sign the paper, Todd," he ordered.

Todd shook his head. "No. I won't sign it."

"Todd!" his mother cried out.

"It's not true! I won't sign it."

Todd's father grabbed the pen and tried to put it back in Todd's hand. Nolan stood up.

"That's all right. Let him suffer the consequences," he said. He walked around his desk to stand in front of Todd. "You think you can save Mr. Keating?" Nolan asked. "You saw it, boy, we have the signatures of all the others. But, if you don't sign, you're on disciplinary probation for the rest of the year. You'll do work duty every afternoon and every weekend. And, if you set foot off campus, you'll be expelled."

Todd's parents and Mr. Nolan watched Todd, waiting for him to change his mind. Todd sat silent.

"I won't sign," he said softly but firmly.

"Then I'll see you back here after classes," Nolan said, turning his back. "Leave."

Todd stood and walked out the door. Nolan looked at Todd's parents. "I'm sorry, Mr. Nolan," Mrs. Anderson said. "I can't help but feel this is our fault."

"We never should have sent him here," Mr. Anderson said, looking down at the floor.

"Nonsense," Nolan said. "Boys his age are highly impressionable. We'll bring him around."

The next day, Mr. McAllister led a group of Latin students across the snow-covered campus as they repeated verbs out loud. He stopped and looked up at the teachers' residence floor where he noticed the lonely figure of Mr. Keating, watching out the window. Their eyes met briefly. McAllister turned away, took a deep breath, and resumed walking with the boys.

Keating moved from the window after seeing McAllister. He walked to his bookshelf and started to take down his beloved books of poetry—Byron, Whitman, Wordsworth. He sighed and put them back. Closing his suitcase, he walked to the door of the tiny room, took one last look, and left.

As Keating prepared to leave, his former students were in English class. Todd sat numbly, eyes cast downward, the way he had sat when school first began. Knox, Meeks, and Pitts looked humiliated as they squirmed in their seats. All of the former club members were too ashamed of themselves to even look at one another. Only Cameron appeared halfway normal, studying at his desk as though nothing had happened.

Conspicuously missing from the room were the desks that belonged to Neil and Charlie.

The door opened suddenly and Mr. Nolan walked in. The boys stood. Nolan sat at the teacher's desk, and they all sat down. "I will be taking over this class through exams," Nolan said as he looked around the room. "We will find a permanent English teacher during the break. Who will tell me where you are in the Pritchard textbook?"

Nolan looked around. There were no volunteers. "Mr. Anderson?"

"The . . . Pritchard . . ." Todd repeated, barely audible. He looked through his books, fumbling nervously.

"I can't hear you, Mr. Anderson," Nolan said.

"I . . . think . . . we . . ." Todd said, still speaking softly.

"Mr. Cameron," Nolan said, exasperated by Todd's response, "kindly inform me."

"We skipped around a lot, sir. We covered the romantics and some of the chapters on post–Civil War literature."

"What about the realists?" Nolan asked

"I believe we skipped most of that," Cameron said.

Nolan stared at Cameron and then looked around the class. "All right then, we'll start over. What is poetry?" He waited for an answer. No one volunteered. Suddenly the door to the classroom opened, and Mr. Keating walked in.

"I came for my personals," he said to Nolan. "Should I wait until after class?"

"Get your things, Mr. Keating," Nolan said testily. He turned to the class. "Gentlemen, turn to page 21 of the introduction. Mr. Cameron, read aloud the excellent essay by Dr. Pritchard on understanding poetry."

"Mr. Nolan, that page has been ripped out," Cameron said.

"Then borrow somebody else's book," Nolan said, losing his patience.

"They're all ripped out, sir," Cameron reported.

Nolan stared at Keating. "What do you mean they're all ripped out?"

"Sir, we . . ." Cameron started.

"Never mind, Cameron," Nolan said. He handed his textbook to Cameron. "Read!" he ordered.

"'Understanding Poetry' by Dr. J. Evans Pritchard, PhD. 'To fully understand poetry, we must first be fluent with its meter, rhyme, and figures of speech, then ask two questions: 1) how artfully has the objective . . .'"

As Cameron continued reading, Keating stood at the closet in the corner of the room, looking at the students. He saw Todd, whose eyes were full of tears. He saw Knox, Meeks, Pitts . . . still too ashamed to look him in the eye, but nevertheless, full of emotion. He sighed. The irony of Nolan's choosing the Pritchard essay just as he walked in the room was just too incredible. He finished packing and walked across the room toward the door. Just as Keating reached the door, Todd jumped up.

"Mr. Keating," he cried out, interrupting Cameron's reading.

"They made everybody sign it!"

Nolan stood up angrily. "Quiet, Mr. Anderson," he ordered.

"Mr. Keating," Todd continued, "it's true. You have to believe me!"

"I believe you, Todd," Keating said softly.

Nolan was enraged. "Leave, Mr. Keating!" he shouted.

"But it wasn't his fault, Mr. Nolan!" Todd refused to stop.

Nolan rushed down the aisle and pushed Todd back into his seat. "Sit down, Mr. Anderson!" he shouted. "One more outburst from you . . ." He turned toward the rest of the class. "Or anyone else, and you are out of this school!" Nolan turned toward Keating, who had stepped back into the room toward Todd, as though to help. "Leave, Mr. Keating!" he shrieked. "Now!"

The boys stared at Keating. He stared back at them, taking them all in for the last time. Then he turned and walked toward the door.

"O Captain! My Captain!" Todd called out. Keating turned to look at Todd. The rest of the class turned, too. Todd propped one foot up on his desk, hoisted himself up onto it, and, fighting back tears, faced Mr. Keating.

"Sit down," Nolan yelled as he moved toward Todd.

As Nolan started down the aisle toward him, Knox, on the other side of the room, called out Mr. Keating's name and stood up on his desk too. Nolan turned toward Knox. Meeks mustered up his courage and stood up on his desk. Pitts did the same. One by one, and then in groups, others in the class followed their lead, standing on their desks in silent salute to Mr. Keating.

Nolan gave up trying to control the class and stood motionless, staring in amazement at this overwhelming tribute to the former English teacher.

Keating stood at the door, overcome with emotion. "Thank you, boys," he said. "I . . . thank you." Keating looked into Todd's eyes, then into the eyes of all the Dead Poets. He nodded, then turned and walked out the door, leaving them standing on their desks in silent salute.